the IMPOSSIBLE DESTINY of CUTIE GRACKLE

Published by
PEACHTREE PUBLISHING COMPANY INC.
1700 Chattahoochee Avenue
Atlanta, Georgia 30318-2112
PeachtreeBooks.com

Text © 2022 by Shawn K. Stout
Cover and interior illustrations © 2022 by Alona Millgram

Edited by Catherine Frank
Cover design by Kate Gartner & Adela Pons
Interior design and typeset by Lily Steele

Printed and bound in February 2022 at Thomson Reuters, Eagan, MN, USA.
10 9 8 7 6 5 4 3 2 1
First Edition
ISBN 978-1-68263-320-5

Catalog-in-Publication Data is available from the Library of Congress

the IMPOSSIBLE DESTINY of CUTIE GRACKLE

SHAWN K. STOUT

PEACHTREE
ATLANTA

For Opal and Andy, who taught me
to never lose heart,

and for Yaz, who told me
to listen to the birds.

I would like to paint
the way a bird sings.

—CLAUDE MONET

CHAPTER 1

THE BIRDS WERE FOLLOWING ME.

Which was a very irregular thing, even for me. My life was full of the kinds of things people might call irregular, but up until then, not one of them had to do with birds. I knew it could only mean one thing: Either I stunk of worms, or something bad was fixin' to happen.

In my heart of hearts, I was really hoping for worms.

I was sitting in the front seat of Toot Jefferson's old pickup truck, watching the trees fly by the window, when I spotted the birds for the third time that morning. They were ravens. Five of them.

"One of these days, I'm going to take me a tropical vacation," said Toot. "When I get lucky."

"When will that be?" I asked, sniffing my bare arm and trying to remember the last time I washed.

"Oh, I don't know the particulars," she said, "but one of these days my ship will come in. Believe you me."

I stuck my head out of the window to get a better look at the birds. The warm June wind tickled my face. They were doing a pretty fine job of keeping up with us, those birds. Although, considering how tenderfooted Toot was with the gas pedal, it couldn't have been awful hard. "But there aren't any ports in West Virginia," I said, leaning back inside the truck. That was the problem with living in a landlocked state; there was no easy way out.

"A minor technicality." Toot was gripping the top of the steering wheel with both hands. Each of her plump fingers was outfitted with a ring, which she clacked against the wheel. *Clack. Clack.* "I read about a woman who woke up one morning with the firmly held belief that she would win the lottery even though she had never gambled before in all her life. So she bought herself a ticket. And the next thing she knew, she was a super-mega jackpot winner and on the front page of all the papers. Now she owns a chain of islands. Not just one island, *a whole chain.* Can you believe such a thing?"

I nodded.

I believed in most impossible things.

Toot steered her old truck over the dips in the gravel road down the mountain. Her dyed curls, the color of a chili pepper, swept her chin. The road to the nearest town, Gypsum, was steep, and Toot badgered the brake the whole way.

Toot Jefferson worked in the cafeteria at Vera B. Marigold Elementary, where I had just finished fifth grade. Toot saw it as her own personal concern to look in on me, especially during the summer, and once a month, she drove me down to Gypsum's No Hunger Food Pantry, where I could get food for myself and my uncle, Horace.

"Do you see those birds behind us?" I said, looking out the window again.

"Birds?" Toot adjusted her rearview mirror.

"I think they're following me," I said. "I saw them back at Horace's place, and now here they are again."

"Following you?" said Toot. She clobbered the brakes, sending me into the dashboard.

"Murderation!" I said, shifting back into my seat and holding on to the door handle.

Then Toot gave me a worried look. "Honey, birds don't follow. They look for food. They build nests. They lay eggs. Such is the uncomplicated life of a bird. We should all be so lucky." She frowned and kept her eyes on me until I looked away.

Maybe I'm getting like Horace, I thought as I watched the trees out my window. *Strange. Or, sick.*

"Now then," Toot said, easing off the brake for a bit and then smashing it again. "How's it been?"

I tugged at a loose thread on the cuff of my jeans. "There's something wrong with Horace." Toot raised her eyebrows at me, and I said, "I mean, more wrong than usual. Lately all he does is sleep. Unless he's running around with Charlie Mullet. He was gone three days and then came back last night, muttering to himself about the curse again. And sometimes, he just stares out the window, you know? At nothing. Like he's here, but he's not really here. Like his mind is caught someplace else."

Clack. Clack.

Uncle Horace had always been strange, since as far back as I could remember. Strange because he kept himself away from most people, and he never was much for talking. When he did have something to say, he didn't make a whole lot of sense. He talked in circles, and even triangles and rectangles, but never in straight lines. He believed that a curse was set on him and our family, and that's the reason we lived the way we did, him and me. The reason my parents went away. He wouldn't say anything more about the curse than that, not that I believed him much, anyhow.

Over the years, I'd gotten used to Horace and his strange ways, but the last couple of weeks, ever since Charlie Mullet came back around, something was different. It was like there was a curtain pulled tight around Horace that kept him in a dark place, that kept him from being in the world that everybody else lived in, including mine.

"I don't mean that old Horace," said Toot, shaking her head. "I mean *you*, sugar. How's it been?"

Clack. Clack.

"Oh. Fine." The words came out as thin as toilet paper. Still, I nodded, smiled, and hoped Toot would believe they were true. Nothing good would come from Toot worrying any more than she already did.

"One day you'll see," she said, taking her foot off the brake and letting the truck catch some speed. "Your life's gonna change in a heartbeat. Just that quick."

Toot said that a lot. But it couldn't happen quick enough for me.

I looked in the truck's side mirror. The ravens were still there.

We hit a deep pothole. I bobbed in my seat, and the coil springs underneath me sproinged.

Toot pushed up her purple glasses and rubbed at the deep lines in her forehead, smoothing them. "Sugar, I've got to tell you something. I'm going away for a little while."

Clack. Clack.

Something heavy pulled at my stomach. "Away?" I sputtered. "Where? For how long?"

Then Toot explained that her mama had gotten worse and how she was going to be with her on her last days. *Last days*, that's what she said. She was going to drive all night, the good Lord willing, across the great state of West Virginia to Charles Town, where her mother lived. She didn't know how long she would be gone. Maybe a few weeks. Maybe more.

The trees that lined both sides of the road leaned in closer, as if they couldn't believe it either.

I wrapped the loose thread from my jeans tight around my finger. Like I was holding on to the world and trying to steer it around a bend. "Can I come with you?"

"You know I would bring you along if I could," answered Toot. She tramped on the brakes again. "I don't think Horace would like it."

"We could ask him," I said.

Toot shook her head. "It's not only that, sugar. My mama, she's so sick." Her voice grew smaller. "She's about to leave this world, and the manner in which she's gonna do that may not be something you want to see."

I didn't want to see anybody leave this world, but the problem was, I also didn't want Toot to leave mine. The wind untucked my hair from behind my ear.

Toot reached over and put it back into place. "You know if I had my druthers, the way things are for you right now, well, that's not the way things would be."

I let go of the thread. *Would be.* It was an idea so big I couldn't see its edges, and nothing was too impossible to fit inside. Like waking up one day and, just like that, finding that everything was different. Easier.

We were quiet for a long time.

"My mama," said Toot, after a while. "She liked to tell me fairy stories when I was a little girl about your age. Sometimes the stories came from a book, but most of the time, I think she just made them up on the spot. But before she got going with a story, she always told me to keep my eye on the luminaries."

"What are luminaries?"

"That's the same thing I asked her," said Toot. "She told me that luminaries are the bright ones. The ones who look into the belly of the dark forest and see a way through when nobody else can. By the end, some of them even made it to the highfalutin castle. And you, Cutie Grackle, you've got the makings of a luminary. You've just got to do what I'm always telling you."

"Don't lose heart," I replied.

"Amen to that."

CHAPTER 2

AT THE BOTTOM OF THE MOUNTAIN, TOOT MADE A SLOW TURN into the parking lot of Gypsum's No Hunger Food Pantry. There was an empty parking space between two bigger trucks near the front door, and Toot lined up her truck to back into it. "Easy as threading a needle," she said as she threw the pickup into reverse and fixed her eyes on the rearview mirror.

Toot and I met when I was in the first grade at Vera B. Marigold Elementary. She was the one who had signed me up for the Calhoun County Schools Student Nutrition Services program after a couple of girls with pink hair ribbons had complained that I spent the lunch hour staring at the food on their trays. (In all fairness, I would have been happy to stare at the food on my own tray if I'd had one.) Those girls' complaints were delivered in the form of chocolate milk blown at me through a straw. I had caught some of the milk on my tongue, and it tasted so good, I wished for another blast.

But that was something I never told those girls.

After the bell rang, Toot had given me a paper napkin for my face and then sat next to me, patting my hand as she talked. It was the first time anyone had been that close that I could remember. And for certain the first time anyone had held my hand. I felt as if someone had plugged me into an electrical socket, and I lit up like a lamp.

"It makes them a bit goosey," Toot had explained to me in a whisper. "Your being a little different and all. But they don't know what they don't know. And what they don't know is a lot. There ain't no crime in being poor." She brought her face close to mine and met my eyes. Toot smelled like sunshine and orange soda.

Although the Calhoun County Schools Student Nutrition Services program meant that I could get breakfast and lunch during the school year without having to pay for them, Toot had said that even they weren't really *free*. "Everything in this world comes with a price," she'd said. "Somebody always has to pay."

During the summer months, my only food came from the pantry. It wasn't nearly enough to keep from being hungry, but if everything came with a price to pay, maybe that was mine.

Gypsum's No Hunger Food Pantry was a small, gray cement-block building that used to be a Super Shoes, and before that Kiki's House of Tacos, and before that Chaz Hawtrey's Party Supply Store. It was the kind of place that didn't know what it was supposed to be.

I understood that kind of place.

Before climbing out of the truck, I looked out the window for the ravens. They were gone. Maybe Toot was right. Maybe they hadn't been following me after all.

Maybe they were just birds doing bird things.

I grabbed the cardboard box behind my seat and followed Toot inside.

CHAPTER 3

INSIDE GYPSUM'S NO HUNGER FOOD PANTRY, THERE WERE ROWS of metal shelves filled with bread, canned fruits and vegetables, meats, cereals, and baked goods. I showed my Calhoun County food-bank card at the registration table to Miss Prudie, who was the No Hunger Food Pantry volunteer coordinator. She said hello to me and Toot, then handed my card to the woman sitting next to her to be hole-punched. The woman had thin gray hair in tight curls, with a pink elastic headband that divided her head right in the middle like the equator. Her name was Izzy, according to her name tag. And she was new, according to the big blue button pinned on her T-shirt that read "Volunteer in training."

A small metal fan on the table stirred the room's warm air, and every time it directed its aim at Izzy, I caught a whiff of cigarettes and expired milk.

Miss Prudie handed me the sheet of paper with a list of items to choose from.

I had only just touched its very edge before Izzy snatched the paper from my fingers. "Now, you can't just choose anything you please," she said. "There are rules to be followed." Then she started explaining to me what food I was allowed to get, until Miss Prudie told her that I was an old hat and knew the drill.

"I'm a regular," I explained to Izzy, reaching for the paper. "Don't worry, I know what to do."

Izzy frowned at me in such a way that made her lips disappear and said, "I know what *old hat* means. I happen to be one myself." But eventually her lips returned, and she let me have the list.

In Calhoun County, a family of two—which is how the town saw me and Horace, as a *family*, even if I had different ideas—could get sixteen items each month. I looked over the list and checked off what I needed: one loaf of bread, two bags of cereal, three cans of meat (I always chose tuna fish), two bags of rice, four cans of vegetables, three cans of fruit, and one baked good.

While Miss Prudie worked on filling my box with the food from my list, the new volunteer named Izzy fiddled with the hole puncher. "You're awful young to be coming in here, aren't you?" Izzy said.

"I'm ten?" It wasn't a question, even if it came out that way. I *was* ten. Just shy of eleven. And that was old enough to know that there was no such thing as being too young to be hungry. I'd been hungry since I could remember.

"Ten." Izzy clucked her tongue. She looked at my food-bank card and then at me. "Says here somebody named Horace is head of household and the proprietor of this here card. And neither of you look like a Horace to me."

"It's all right," called Miss Prudie from behind the shelf of hot-dog buns. "I can vouch for this one."

"He's my uncle," I offered, trying to explain, even though Horace was beyond explanation. *He isn't right in his mind. He took care of us the best he could for a long time, but now I can't count on him to take care of much at all. Lately it feels like I am the grown-up, and he is the kid.*

Those were the explanations about Horace that I went over in my head, but I decided only to say, "I'm head of household when it comes to food."

"Is that right," said Izzy, raising her eyebrows.

"This girl's an old soul," said Toot, giving my shoulder a squeeze.

"You don't say."

Miss Prudie asked Toot about her mama's health, and Toot left me to go talk with her.

I watched Izzy as she turned over my card, reading the fine print on the back about eligibility and terms of use. There was a rule about not giving food to anyone except the person whose name was on the card, but most of the other volunteers knew about my situation with Horace, or guessed at it, and they were willing to bend that rule.

Izzy didn't seem like the kind of lady who bent things. She turned the card back over and held it about an inch from her eyes. "Your uncle lives on Smite Mountain. Is that right?"

"Yes, ma'am," I said. "I do too. I mean, I live with him."

"And what about your parents? They're not in the

picture?" Izzy lowered the card and then looked right at me. Directly into my eyeballs.

I didn't know what business this was of hers, anyway, or what sort of picture she was talking about. There weren't any pictures of my parents that I ever saw. My mama's name was Magda, I knew that much about her, and she was Horace's sister. I didn't know anything about my father. The times I had asked Horace about my parents, he told me they were cursed, just like him, and they weren't coming back so there was no use in blubbering about what never would be.

Never would be. I hated the very idea.

"They went away when I was a baby," I told the lady. I didn't mention the curse.

"Ain't that a shame," said Izzy. "Some people aren't cut out to be parents, I guess."

My face filled up with heat. *This lady doesn't even know my parents. This lady who smells like spoiled milk and cigarettes. This lady who has disappearing lips. What does she know about anything?*

I tried to catch Toot's eye, but she and Miss Prudie were whispering in a huddle by the canned peas.

"You know, I've lived in Gypsum my whole life," said Izzy. "And I've seen a lot of comings and goings."

When people started sentences with *you know*, they always proceeded to tell you something you didn't. I didn't care for that way of talking. So I didn't say anything and just kept my eyes on the fan. It was rotating from side to side.

"My late husband, Maynard, may he rest in peace, was the sheriff for quite a few years," Izzy said.

It felt like she was waiting for me to say something. I pretended to be very fascinated by the fan.

"He got word of some strange things happening up there on Smite Mountain," Izzy continued, leaning toward me. "You ever hear anything about that?"

It took exactly eight seconds for the fan to change direction. I counted.

"You know," said Izzy, "there were reports of deaths. Freak accidents, you could say, but by the time my Maynard got there to investigate, the bodies were just gone."

I looked at her. "What do you mean *gone*?"

"I mean just what I said. Gone. Disappeared. No trace of them left behind. Maynard always said that mountain was cursed."

I felt a hand on my shoulder then, and I flinched. It was Toot. "You all right, sugar?" she said.

"Fine."

"I was giving this young girlie here a history lesson about that mountain she lives on," Izzy said. "Some kind of curse set on that place up there."

Toot shook her head. "Oh, that's a bunch of phooey." Then she said to me, "You know there's no such thing as curses."

Izzy clucked her tongue and eyeballed Toot. "How long have you lived in Gypsum?"

"About five years," answered Toot.

"Five years." Izzy made a *ppfffffttttt* sound. "That's nothing. The wart on my big toe has been around longer than that. Five years isn't long enough to know anything about anything."

Then something behind me caught Izzy's attention. She leaned to the side and looked over my shoulder.

I turned around. Outside of the window behind me, the ravens had returned. They were perched on the hood of Toot's pickup.

Toot marched to the door, swung it open, and clapped her hands. "Get going, all of you! Shoo!" The birds scattered. "Imagine that, a whole mountain of open land, and these birds want to use my truck as a toilet."

When I looked back at Izzy, she raised her eyebrows at me. Then she picked up the hole puncher and used both hands to punch through the "June" on my card. There was a *pop* from the punch. I flinched again.

Izzy held out the card for me. But before she let go, she said, "I'd be on my guard, if I were you, living up there. Indeed I would. Mark my words."

Toot returned to me and put her hands on my shoulders. "Well, thank you for the . . . history lesson," she said, pulling me toward her and away from Izzy. "It looks like Miss Prudie is just about done. And we best be getting on."

I could feel Izzy's eyes on me as I watched Miss Prudie put the last item into my box. It was a sheet cake with white-and-blue sugar icing. Sometimes a local bakery donated cakes that were never picked up by the people who ordered them. But it hardly ever happened. And I had never gotten such a cake before.

Toot elbowed me. "Jackpot, sugar," she whispered, nodding in the direction of the cake. "Super-mega jackpot."

I stole a quick look at Izzy. Her lips were still gone, and she was staring at me so hard that her glassy eyes nearly went crossed.

"Here you are," said Miss Prudie when she handed me the box. "See you next month."

"Unless my ship comes in," Toot said, ushering me toward the door. "And then I'll be on an island."

I looked back at Izzy one last time. She stabbed her finger in my direction and mouthed, "Mark my words."

CHAPTER 4

I CLIMBED INTO THE PASSENGER SEAT OF TOOT'S PICKUP AND WEDGED the box of food between my legs. "Do you think that could be true?" I said.

"What?" said Toot, pumping the gas pedal until the truck's engine caught.

"What that Izzy lady said about all the freak accidents and disappearances on Smite Mountain. Maybe that's the curse that Horace has been talking about."

Toot wrinkled her nose. "People in this town do a lot of talking about curses, you know that. When the coal mine shut down, I bet the whole town went catty-wampus. It's plumb easier to blame hard times on a curse. When people can't make heads or tails about why things are the way they are."

"But do you *think* it could be true?" I asked again. There were miles and miles between *thinking* and *believing*, or at least there seemed to be. "I mean, how could people just disappear like she said?"

Toot grinned and said in a spooky voice, "Maybe it was the Mothman or the Snarly Yow."

"I'm serious," I said. Some people believed that monsters like the Mothman or the Snarly Yow or the White Creature roamed the West Virginia hills. Even though I believed in most impossible things, I didn't believe in monsters. Not that kind, anyway.

"Look," said Toot, "like I told you, I don't much believe in curses. It goes against my general philosophy that I'm the boss of my own life. Which I most certainly, one hundred percent am. You go believing in curses and the next thing you know, you start believing that somebody else is in charge of you."

Toot put the truck in gear, and in one snort of the engine, we were out of the parking space and onto Purder Road heading back up the mountain.

I still wasn't convinced. "Maybe . . ."

"Maybe what?" Toot said.

"Maybe my parents didn't leave to find work some-place else. Maybe they really were cursed. Maybe they disappeared." It's not that I wanted to believe this was true, but it was something. And when you knew next to nothing about the reasons your parents left you behind, *something* was worth considering. *Something* was all you had.

"Sugar, that lady back there was pulling your leg. Don't let your imagination take hold. Curses aren't real. And there's no point in worrying about things that aren't real when there are plenty of real things to be worrying about." She steered the truck onto Smite Run. "Now, let's talk about that cake."

Before I knew it, we were at the end of Smite Run and barreling onto the dirt lane that led to Horace's. He and I lived in a shack that teetered on the edge of the world. It was built high atop a steep cliff that over-looked a gorge. Gypsum was fifteen miles down the mountain. The nearest neighbor, same.

You couldn't see Horace's shack from the road on account of the thick pines and overgrowth of bittersweet. People might drive right on by and never know we were living back there. Or maybe they wouldn't want to know in the first place.

The shack, which had been patched together with old fencing, rusted metal siding, and used car parts, had a pronounced and curious lean. Like it was peering over the cliff to see what was down below. But when a breeze came across the mountain, it would lose its nerve, and the whole thing, in one loud creak, would shift back toward the land.

Toot and I were halfway down the dirt lane when the shack came into view, along with Horace. He stepped off the porch and was looking up at the sky, shielding his eyes from the sun.

Toot brought the truck around and came to a stop between him and the porch. "Gracious almighty," said Toot. "Doesn't he look worse for wear."

Horace was tall and sickly thin. Considering all the dirt that clung to him, you might think he washed himself in mud, but the truth was, these last few weeks, he rarely washed at all. His whiskers were patchy, and his dark hair was stringy, long, and so full of grease that it looked wet.

I felt Toot's eyes on me, and for some reason, I was ashamed for Toot to see him this way. Like somehow it was my fault, since I'm the only one he has to look after him. "I didn't have a chance to give him a haircut this week," I explained. "Or a shave."

Toot put her truck in park and said again, "Gracious almighty." This time it came out in a whisper and sounded like a prayer.

I unbuckled my seatbelt and held my breath, forcing myself to get out of the truck. It's not that I was afraid of my uncle. I wasn't. But lately, being around him made me feel uneasy. As if my insides were made of knots.

Charlie Mullet, Horace's only friend (if you could call him that), was a different story. When he was around, those knots inside of me got pulled real tight, and I got the urge to run.

I never could figure why Horace let him come around, because Charlie was meaner than a wet hen. He had a pointy chin that jutted out sharp, and his face was as unfriendly as a lizard's. And there was something else too: The way Charlie looked at me. It was like he hated me. I didn't know why.

Before I got out of the truck, I made sure Charlie's van wasn't parked anywhere nearby. Toot let the motor run and came around to my side of the truck to help me take the box of food up the stairs to the porch.

"Uncle Horace," I hollered, setting the box on the wooden porch floor. "I'm back. I'll make us some lunch."

Horace turned to look at me and Toot, but he didn't say anything. Then he turned away from us and looked up at the sky again. *What is he doing?*

Seeing Horace there like he was, and knowing that Toot was leaving, gave me an awful, sick feeling. I pushed against the box with my shoe, denting a corner. "Why do you have to go?" I asked Toot, already knowing the answer.

"Cutie . . ."

I didn't let her finish. I felt a gush of anger rise up into my throat and then sting my eyes. "I don't understand why I can't come with you."

Toot reached for my hand, but I jerked it away. The knots inside of me were pulled tight. They were the only thing holding me together. I knew if she patted my hand, they'd come undone.

"Forget it." I crossed my arms over my chest and looked at the ground. Then I blurted out, "Well, I hope you have fun with your mom." As soon as I said it, the anger drained right out of me. Shame took its place. Toot wasn't going to have fun. Her mother was dying. I knew that. But still, it was me being left alone.

I wanted to take it back. But sometimes the things you wanted were impossible to get. So I didn't say anything else.

I tried not to feel her eyes on me. Tried not to think how she said I've got the makings of a luminary. Tried not to hear her voice crack when she leaned close and whispered, "All right, then. Be good now. And don't lose heart."

I turned away and didn't watch her get back into her truck. I couldn't make myself.

When I looked back at last, Toot had already disappeared down the lane in a cloud of dust.

Only Horace was left standing there when the dust cleared. He was still watching the sky.

I saw them then. The ravens. Five black specks against the blue sky. They were headed for the tree line, just beyond the lane.

CHAPTER
5

"**B**IRDS DON'T FOLLOW," I TOLD MYSELF, REPEATING WHAT TOOT HAD told me. From the porch, I watched the five ravens circle close to the tree line and then disappear into the canopy.

Horace was still watching them.

"They build nests," I said. "They lay eggs. They don't follow." I spun the doorknob, which was a steering wheel from an old Ford. Then I pushed open the door with my foot and slid the box of food across the porch and into the shack. There were only two rooms inside. Mine and Horace's, at opposite ends, with a tiny kitchen and washroom on Horace's side.

In between my room and Horace's was another

door. It opened to the three-hundred-foot drop into the gorge below. For the kind of reasons having to do with plummeting to your death, we kept this door locked.

I divided the cans into four neat rows on the small shelf in the kitchen. It was a system I made up. Each row had a week's worth of food in it, and if I stuck to the system and stayed in my week of food, then I wouldn't run out before it was time to go back to the pantry.

I opened the plastic lid to the cake, and my stomach got all growly. "Oh, Lordy, Look Who's Forty!" was written in bright-blue sugar icing across the center, and sugary roses sprouted out of each corner. I cut myself a piece big enough to fit a rose and the words "Oh, Lordy" and put the rest in the cupboard along with the bread.

I wondered what it would be like to get as old as forty, and if I'd forget to do things like pick up my birthday cake from the bakery. Then I licked off the blue icing and felt sorry for eating someone else's cake. But only a little sorry and not too much, because it was the absolute best thing my tongue had ever tasted. When I finished, I made myself half of a tuna-fish sandwich and took it to my room.

My room wasn't very big, but that was okay with me because I didn't have much to put in it, anyhow. It fit my bed, which was the back seat of a 1969 Chevrolet Bel Air, and a wooden three-drawer dresser. The only other things I had were a kerosene lamp, a grapevine basket, and a book about the painter Claude Monet called *The Enchanted Tales of French Impressionism.* It was the one book in Horace's place, and who knows where it came from because Horace didn't read. Or maybe he couldn't. I never asked.

I'd read the book all the way through eight times. Claude Monet was a madman who sometimes took a knife to his canvases and set them on fire. But his paintings, the ones that didn't go up in flames—they were like dreams. And I wanted to live inside them.

I was two bites into my sandwich when I heard the groan of the front door and then the creak of the pine floorboards under heavy boots. Horace.

I opened my door.

Horace was leaning against the wall. He wiped his eyes with the back of his hand.

"I got us some food at the pantry," I said. "Miss Prudie even stuck in somebody's birthday cake."

"They've come again," he muttered. "For one more."

"Who's come again?" I said. "Uncle Horace? What's the matter?"

He continued muttering, but I couldn't understand him. I went to the kitchen and grabbed a clean mug next to the sink basin. The mug had a blue monster wearing sunglasses painted on the side, and above the monster in bubble letters were the words "Good Things Happen."

I filled the mug with water from the pump over the basin and carried it to Horace.

I came up to the middle of his T-shirt where there was a grease stain in the shape of a swan. Horace didn't seem to notice me standing in front of him, and probably the swan didn't either. I cleared my throat and waited. "Here," I said, holding out the mug. "Drink this."

Horace blinked. Then he looked at me like he was surprised to see me, or didn't recognize me, or maybe both things at once. "Charlie won't like this. He'll be mad. It's so dark now," he whimpered. "Not like it used to be, before . . ." His voice trailed off.

"Come on. Here." I put the mug of water in his hand. His dirty fingers were trembling.

I helped him bring the mug to his mouth. A good bit dribbled down his whiskered chin.

"Not like it used to be before what?" I said, hoping that he might tell me something for once. Something that made sense. "Uncle Horace?"

He blinked again. Then his eyes got wide, and his mouth fell open. He dropped the mug of water. It hit the floor and broke into pieces that went flying across the room.

Horace stumbled to his bedroom while I stared at the pieces of the mug on the floor. The monster was broken in half, but it was still smiling. The piece with "Good" on it was in the kitchen. "Things Happen" landed on the toe of my shoe.

I gathered up some of the broken pieces and tried to fit them together, but there were too many. *All the king's horses and all the king's men couldn't put Humpty together again.* Those words from that old nursery rhyme popped into my head. If there were some things so broken that even the king's horses and the king's men couldn't fix them, honestly, what hope was there for the rest of us?

In the time it took me to sweep up the pieces, dry the floor with a towel, and use the washroom, Horace was dead asleep. His snores were so loud, it sounded like a bunch of dump trucks had been shoved up his nose.

I went outside and sat on the steps of the small porch. I watched the shadows reach across the mountain and the sun dip behind it. For some reason, on especially hot days, and when the wind was right, the mountain air smelled sweet and sugary, like pancake syrup. It smelled that way right then. I breathed in the air, and my mouth watered.

All of a sudden came the low, croaking calls of birds. I heard them before I could see them.

They weren't there, and then they were. Just that quick.

There were five, like before, not more than a couple of feet in front of me. Ravens. Up close they were the biggest birds I'd ever seen. From beak to tail about the size of a woodchuck and black as motor oil. One hopped even closer to me. It had something sticking out of its very pointy black beak. Something small and white.

The bird cocked its head and gave me a look like it was waiting for me to say something. What did you say to ravens who were following you? *Please don't peck me to death* was the first thing that came into my head. But

"I'm not a worm" is what I decided on. Then just to make sure, I sniffed at my arm and my armpit. Sweat and tuna fish, maybe, but not worms. Come to think of it, I wasn't so sure ravens were the kind of birds that ate worms. Maybe they ate bigger things. Dead things. Like squirrels. Did I smell like a dead squirrel?

The raven turned its head, and only then I noticed that one of its eyes was completely gone. Black, matted feathers covered the sunken socket where the eye should've been.

"I'm sorry about your eye," I said. "What happened?"

The bird opened its beak. It was all so strange that I thought for a second it was going to answer. Instead, the small and white thing fell out of its mouth, and the sweet mountain air gave it enough of a push so that it came to rest beside my shoe.

I picked it up.

It was a fortune. The kind that came from inside a cookie.

What was written on it was this: "History is not your destiny. Uncover your destiny, and you will remake history."

CHAPTER 6

A S SOON AS I READ THE WORDS, A JOLT OF ELECTRICITY SHOT FROM my fingers all the way up my arm and prickled right to my chest. Then, all at once, everything that had been right in front of my eyes seconds before—the birds, the porch steps, the mountain, the fortune—began to blur around the edges and slowly fade away.

Like candy melting on my tongue.

In place of the birds, the porch steps, the mountain, and the fortune, something else began to take form. I blinked hard a couple of times to make sure my eyes were working right. Moments later, I could see a bedroom. I saw it plain as day. The room was dark and full of shadows, and there was a four-poster bed right in front of me. Pale-blue moonlight beamed in through the tall window and shined onto a lump under the bedcovers. *Where am I?* is what I wanted to shout, but I didn't dare because the lump, whoever it was, might not take kindly to me being there in the middle of the night. And I couldn't really blame them.

Is this real? I thought. Stepping closer to the bed, I stuck out my hand to touch the blanket, but before I could, a raven flew in from the open window and perched on the wooden headboard. It was the one-eyed raven. It made knocking sounds at the lump.

Three other ravens were perched on the window-sill, watching.

The lump sat up in bed. It was a young woman. She had short dark hair and freckles across her cheeks. She looked familiar. Like somebody I should know.

Like somebody I wanted to know.

And not only that, she looked a lot like me.

"I knew you were coming, and I know why you're here," the woman said to the one-eyed bird. Then she looked past me to the far corner of the dark room. In that corner was a baby making dribbling noises in a crib.

A baby.

The raven flew from the headboard onto the empty pillow beside the woman. The bird held a slip of white paper in its beak and dropped it gently into the woman's lap. She read the words on the paper out loud: "History is not your destiny. Uncover your destiny, and you will remake history." *The same fortune that the birds brought me.*

The woman looked at the raven and nodded. Like she understood something.

Then she climbed out of bed and came toward me. I said, "Murderation! I'm not sure how I got here, but—" and I backed up to get out of her way, but she passed right through me without saying anything, without even seeing me. That's when I realized that she couldn't hear me and she couldn't see me because I wasn't really there. I was just watching it happen.

Like I was inside a memory.

I watched the woman pick up her baby from the crib and fasten it in a harness to her front. Then she threw a raincoat over her nightdress and buttoned the coat around them both. Its silver buttons were shaped like anchors, I noticed, and her nervous fingers fumbled over them.

She left the room and went down the hall. I followed. She pushed open a door to another room and peeked in. There was a young man asleep in his bed. His covers were balled up tight in his fists like he was holding on for dear life, and in between dump-truck snores, he was whimpering. Like he was being haunted by a terrible, terrible dream.

Is that Horace?

The woman stood in the doorway and ducked her head into the opening of her raincoat. She whispered to her baby, "We've lost so much. First Grandma Pearlie Mae, then Mother and Pa. But don't you worry, Cutie. I'm going to make it right."

I wasn't sure if I had ever felt a sound before, or if it was even possible to *feel* a sound, but that's what happened: I felt her say my name just then. It felt like holding on and letting go at the same time.

As soon as she said it, I knew.

The baby was me. And the young woman, she was my mama.

Everything began to fade away then. "No," I said, reaching out, because I wanted her to stay. I wanted to hear my mama say my name again. There were a few seconds of darkness, and then she came back. This time, she was on a bicycle in the rain, staring at a ramshackle rancher. She pointed a flashlight at a rusted mailbox on a crooked post. The name "Mullet" was in runny-paint letters.

Mullet? What is my mama doing at Charlie Mullet's house?

The full moon was high in the night sky, watching. Waiting for something to happen.

She leaned the bicycle against the house. Then she put one hand on her baby's head—my head—and knocked on the door with the flashlight. After waiting for about a minute, she tried the doorknob. It was unlocked. She pushed open the door and made her way inside. She crept through the front room, which was packed tight with old furniture—chairs with the stuffing spilling out from the cushions, and a bunch of desks, tables, and dressers with broken legs, missing drawers, and peeling paint. Between the stacks of furniture was a narrow pathway that led to the rest of the house.

She started down a long, windowless hallway. I followed and watched as she opened a door at the far end of the hall. She swung her flashlight across the room. There was one piece of furniture—a wooden cabinet stained black with painted gold trim that took up a whole wall, from the floor all the way to the ceiling. The top half of the cabinet was fitted with glass-doored cupboards. Below the cupboards were rows of narrow drawers.

She started opening the drawers. Inside were what looked to me like old axes and heavy stones shaped into spears. There were tiny skulls of animals too.

She moved on to the cupboards next. *What is she looking for?* Behind one glass door were rows of old clay pots. They were stained with dirt like they'd been dug up from the depths of the earth. Most were completely whole with only a few cracks, but it looked like some had been put back together with broken pieces.

Taxidermy animals—squirrels, groundhogs, foxes—peered out through other doors. Next to them were rows of glass jars filled with old beads and wooden pipes carved with faces of animals and people. *Where did all of this stuff come from?*

Then something in a low cupboard got my mama's attention. She let out a gasp. The baby started to cry.

She unlatched the door and pulled out a wooden box. It was next to a taxidermy opossum with an alarmed look on its face.

The box had a "C" carved on its lid.

"Charlie Mullet," she whispered.

She opened the lid.

The baby stopped crying.

After that, my mama and the box with Charlie's initial on it faded away, and I was back on Horace's porch, holding the fortune in my hands, with five ravens watching me.

I rubbed my head, trying to make sense of what I'd just seen. And make sense of the holding-on-and-letting-go feeling that I had.

"That was my—"

I couldn't say the word out loud. It was too full. Too heavy. It got caught in my throat.

Mama.

There was a flutter in my chest. Like my heart was being tickled with a feather.

I didn't expect to look so much like her. Same dark hair. Same freckles. Except instead of brown eyes like mine, hers were blue.

I looked straight at the one-eyed bird. "Did *you* show me that?"

Some of the ravens preened their feathers, and others pecked curiously at the ground. Which I took to mean, *Of course we did, foolish girl.*

"But how?" I said. "What's it supposed to mean? And why was my mama taking something from Charlie?"

The one-eyed bird lowered its head like it was disappointed. Like it had been counting on me to know. Then all at once, the birds took to the air, heading toward the woods where they came from.

I read the fortune again. This time, I ran my thumb over the letters printed on the white paper. And when I did, I felt a heartbeat.

The girl didn't understand. How could I have been clearer? The fortune says it all.

History is not your destiny. Uncover your destiny, and you will remake history.

Destiny. *There is no word with more brilliance and shine. Its lure is unmatched.*

And the heartbeat. She felt it, I'm certain of that.

Ten years ago, the child's mother understood its meaning. Magda understood what was needed to break the curse.

But this girl.

What more needed to be explained? It's really quite simple. Even for a human's mind.

And they call us birdbrained.

CHAPTER 7

COULDN'T HELP IT; I WAS SO GOBSTRUCK BY THE HEARTBEAT AND
what I saw that I dropped the fortune. It drifted down
slowly like a feather and landed on the wooden porch step
below me. Lying there, it didn't look like the kind of thing
to have a beating heart. It looked like the kind of thing
that you'd throw away without thinking twice. Like a
chewing-gum wrapper or a receipt for a bar of soap.

I wondered where the birds had found it.

There was one Chinese restaurant in all of Gypsum:
Darryl's All-You-Can-Eat China Buffet and Subs. You
could get wontons and hoagies. Chicken lo mein and
meatball subs. Toot took me there once for my eighth
birthday. Two fortune cookies had come with the bill,

but when I opened mine, there was nothing inside. Toot felt so miserable about it, she gave me hers. The fortune in her cookie was something like, "If you look back, you'll soon be going that way." I ate the cookie but didn't keep the fortune. I didn't really understand it, and besides that, it was hers to begin with.

"What does this mean?" I said out loud to this fortune, because if it had a heartbeat, it might also have ears and maybe would answer.

It didn't.

Carefully, I picked up the slip of paper, holding on to the very ends. Then, slowly, I closed my hand over the words. The heart was still beating, but this time, the memory did not come.

I squeezed the paper tighter, willing the jolt of electricity to come back. So that I could see my mama again. See her holding me. Hear her say my name.

Nothing.

Only the heartbeat. Its murmur was steady and soothing. Like sitting in a rocking chair. Or holding hands with Toot.

I read the words again. *Destiny*. The sound of that word had magic in it. As if it belonged with the stars.

As if it were full of impossibilities.

I'd always had the feeling that there was something more for me than this. Something bigger than Horace and the shack and this mountain. That whatever it was—*destiny, maybe?*—it was out there somewhere in the big, wide world, waiting for me to find it, and when I did, well, that's when everything would change. Maybe I would even find my family.

Now, here it was.

In my hand I held a link to my mama and something that the birds wanted me to know. *But what?*

I sat there on the porch, rocking back and forth and back and forth to the rhythm, while I thought about impossible things: destiny and curses, the warm arms of my mama, and heartbeating fortunes and the birds who brought them.

I thought about them until nightfall, when my brain got too tired to think anymore.

The yelling woke me. My eyes flew open. My room was still dark.

"Where is it, Horace?" It was Charlie. His voice was thick and greasy like a piece of undercooked meat.

Something hit the wall outside my door.

I sat up. I tried to make myself as small as I could. Small enough to slide under a penny. "A baby mouse, a walnut, a kernel of corn, a grain of wheat, a piece of dirt, a speck of dust. A baby mouse, a walnut—" Over and over, I told myself to be small.

"Where'd she hide it?" yelled Charlie. "Ten years, I've been looking. You told me she made a map. You told me. We've been all over this mountain, and we ain't found nothing. Ten years! Because of her I . . ."

"I know, Charlie," said Horace. "I did tell you. I did. But . . ."

Something else crashed against my door. I could hear the broken pieces pelting the floor.

I tried to shake off the sleep so that I could think. *Who made a map? And what are they looking for?*

"Where is it, Horace? Think!" Charlie's voice was closer.

"It's so dark now. So dark," Horace whimpered. "I can't remember. And they've come. The birds. They've

47

come. I seen them today. I seen them." Horace said something else then, but I couldn't make it out. I pressed my ear against the wall.

"Shut up about them birds!" yelled Charlie. "All you best be thinking about is that map. The curse is gonna happen again if we don't find it. That woman who does the weather on channel eight said in two nights' time there'd be a Rose Moon! You know the last time that happened, don't you?"

"Ten years," answered Horace.

My hand went to my pants pocket, where the fortune was tucked deep inside.

The curse is real.

The curse is real.

The curse is real.

And the birds have something to do with it.

Charlie growled, and something big slammed against the wall. "Ten years ago, she took it. You owe me now, Horace. Think! Use that worthless brain of yours! I've got until that moon comes to find it!"

"I'm telling you I don't know, don't remember!" cried Horace. "How many times do I gotta tell you? I don't know!"

The walls of the shack trembled.

Then, quiet.

"Maybe your girlie in there has some ideas of where to look," said Charlie.

"Naw, leave Cutie alone," said Horace. His voice was so quiet I could barely make it out.

"What'd you say?" said Charlie. "What'd you say to me, you little punk?"

"Nothing."

"That's what I thought," said Charlie. "Maybe she's just the thing to jog your memory. What do you say? Won't hurt to try, now will it? Well, it won't hurt *me*, anyway."

The pine floors outside my door groaned under his heavy boots.

Something inside me told me to run. I shoved my sneakers onto my bare feet. Then I grabbed my kerosene lamp from my dresser, lit it, and threw open my window. I climbed outside, into the moonlight, and ran as fast as I could for the woods.

Much of the forest—from the tree line nearest Horace's shack all the way to Whistling Creek, which divided the mountain in half—I had mapped out in my mind. How the forest west of the creek seemed to be its own mighty kingdom, making and abiding by its own rules. How the thick canopy kept the floor shaded and managed to keep out most of the rain-drops. How the hemlocks seemed to wear clouds as nightshirts and look down at me from miles above. And how if you were the kind of person who didn't notice things, you might think the pines, elms, and hemlocks all looked the same with their drooping, feathery branches and brown, furrowed trunks. For that sort of person, it would be easy to get turned around and forget which direction you were coming from.

But I was not that sort. A long time ago, Horace had taught me the names of all the trees.

Sometimes I stayed out there all night under the shelter of a rock overhang. I felt safe out there, even in the dark.

Under the giant trees, I was small. I could hide from the world.

The trees would listen for the sound of my foot-steps, and when they heard me coming, they would whisper to one another, *She is here, she is here,* lifting their limbs to invite me inside and then wrapping the wind around me like a ribbon to draw me in. I could disappear in the woods, if I wanted to, and never return. If I let the trees swallow me, I knew they would.

CHAPTER 8

I WAS OUT OF BREATH BY THE TIME I GOT TO MY ROCK SHELTER. It was just beyond a quartz outcropping and hidden by a cluster of hemlocks. I dropped to my knees and crawled inside the opening. Then I snuffed out my kerosene lamp and sat in the pitch black, in case Charlie decided to chase after me.

In the quiet dark, that's when I did some of my best thinking. I tried to remember everything Charlie and Horace had said. *Something happened ten years ago and is about to happen again in two nights' time. When there is a . . . What did Charlie call it? A Rose Moon. Whatever is about to happen, it's because of the curse, and Charlie and Horace are afraid of it, that's for sure.*

They need to find something to stop it. A map, Charlie said.

A map to what?

So that's what Horace and Charlie had been doing. When Horace would disappear with Charlie for days on end, I had figured they were over in Blackstone Quarry, digging for gold, diamonds, or buried treasure. Charlie always had a shovel in his hand or one of those metal detectors that beeped when it hovered over coins buried in the ground, and Horace's boots were always filled with dirt. They were like pirates, the two of them, except without an eye patch or a boat.

But they weren't looking for treasure. They were looking for something else. Is it the wooden box with Charlie's initial on it that my mama found? What was in that box?

All this thinking made a pain start to grow in my head.

I leaned my head against the cold quartz wall of the rock shelter. It was just wide enough that if I sat against one wall and stretched out my legs, my feet could almost touch the other side. It wasn't very tall or deep inside either; sitting down, my head just reached the ceiling, and there was barely enough room to turn myself around. Still, it was everything I needed when there was hiding to be done.

The mountain was quiet.

When I was sure that I hadn't been followed, I ran my hands along the opening of the shelter and reached into the crevice for the burlap sack I'd kept there. I shook out onto my lap what was inside: a nub of beef jerky for emergencies, the blue laminated lunch card for school, and my magic lantern. I switched on the lantern and pointed it at the rock wall. The quartz sparkled in the light.

Toot gave me the lantern last Christmas. On the black box it came in was written *Magic Lantern: Experience Electro Radiant Magic at Your Fingertips* in chunky gold lettering. "Everybody needs a little magic now and again, Cutie Pie," Toot had said as she placed it in my hand.

The "lantern" was a small flashlight. The "magic" was clear glass disks—a princess, a witch, a knight, a bird, and a wolf—that were supposed to come with the lantern. (It said so on the box.) But Toot bought it used at the Gypsum Goodwill where everything was sold as is. Which meant no returns, no refunds; what you get is what you get.

What I got was the flashlight with only one disk—the bird. When you switched on the flashlight and pointed it at the wall, the bird from the disk appeared in a circle of light. Like the moon.

Magic or not, I liked watching the bird, who I pretended had been stolen by the moon and couldn't get away.

I pulled out the fortune from my pocket and felt the steady heartbeat under my thumb. I pointed the flashlight at the words. "Destiny," I said, and my tongue tingled.

In the memory, when the one-eyed raven gave my mama the fortune, she said she knew why the bird had come, and she knew what she had to do. She said she had to make it right.

Make it right.

Make it right.

Was my mama trying to break the curse? Did the birds want her to? Was that her destiny?

I lay down on the dirt floor and aimed my flashlight at the stone ceiling of the rock shelter.

I turned the disk on the flashlight so that the bird on the ceiling moved, like it was trying to fly away.

Always trying. The bird wanted to be free. But it wasn't in the moon's nature to let the bird go.

Now, ten years later, the same raven came to me with the same fortune. The same destiny.

Make it right.

Make it right.

Then the knots inside me tightened when I realized. *My mama didn't make it right. She failed. Had the curse taken her?*

The next morning, when the sun was still below the treetops, my stomach woke me up. Which was a very regular thing. Mr. Desmond had said that stomachs were the toddlers of the human body. Mr. Desmond was my fifth-grade science teacher. He was tall and thin with a big nose and long hair, and he wore wire-rimmed glasses that were perfectly round, just like one of the Beatles used to wear. I could never remember which one.

Mr. Desmond started every class by asking a question. One time he asked, "If a tree falls in the forest, but nobody is around to hear it, does it make a sound?" The other kids in my class shouted out *Yes*! or *No*! and then had a big back-and-forth with the ones who disagreed. Mr. Desmond just listened and smiled while they argued, keeping the right answer to himself.

In class, I never did say what I thought the answer could be because when you told people what you thought, it was like you opened a window inside yourself, and people could look in and see your secrets. I didn't want them to see.

The truth was, I didn't know for sure. I thought Mr. Desmond would tell us at the end of class, but he never did. Maybe he didn't know either.

But Mr. Desmond did know a thing or two about stomachs. He said that stomachs acted like toddlers because they were quick to throw a tantrum when they needed something. And they wouldn't stop their fussing (which they sent by way of chemical messengers to the brain) until they got what they wanted.

I had firsthand experience of this. As of right then, my stomach very much wanted butter, bread, and cake!

I put the flashlight back into the burlap sack and slid it into the crevice.

I started off to Horace's. I kept watch for the ravens, but they didn't come.

When I got to the clearing and could see the shack, I slowed my feet. Charlie's van wasn't parked outside, which was a big relief, so even if Horace was there, I figured he was probably alone and probably asleep.

I took my time climbing the stairs on the porch, listening for voices. Or dump-truck snores. The wind whistled through the gaps in the siding. As quiet as I could, I turned the steering wheel and pushed open the door.

Once inside, I let out the air that I had been holding in. Horace wasn't here.

My stomach grumbled in case I needed a reminder that I was hungry. I didn't.

I went to the kitchen, and that's when I saw: The shelves were empty.

I checked the cupboard. The bread, the cereal, the tuna fish. Everything was gone, gone, gone.

It was Charlie who'd taken it, I was sure of it. He'd taken everything, even the rest of the "Oh, Lordy, Look Who's Forty!" cake. The only things left were three cans of lima beans.

And Horace had let it happen.

I sank to the floor. *That food was supposed to last us for a month. It was all we had. How could Horace have just stood by and let Charlie do this?*

My face and neck got hot. I felt sick and, at the same time, hungry.

Then, after a while, less sick.

Then more hungry.

"Come on, Cutie," I told myself. "Don't lose heart."

The fortune's heartbeat thumped in my front pants pocket. "I know," I told it, "I'm supposed to be uncovering my destiny. But unless I find some food to eat, my destiny won't matter because I'll have starved to death. So unless you can help me find food—"

The heartbeat quieted.

"I figured as much."

I pried open a can of lima beans (*slime-a beans* was more like it), warmed them on the cookstove, and forced them down. They settled my stomach enough so I could think. The shack was quiet, and I closed my eyes so that it would be dark. So that I could do my best thinking. *What am I going to do?*

Toot was all the way to her mother's in Charles Town, and there was no phone to call her or anyone else. She'd be gone for a few weeks or more, and two cans of slime-a beans wouldn't last me that long.

I checked the whole shack. There was nothing else that could pass for food unless you counted the grains of salt and pepper in the shakers on the cookstove. Nothing else, unless I caught a rabbit or a squirrel, like I had seen Horace do so many times. But I'd put off that idea for as long as I could. For one thing, I had never actually trapped an animal, not by myself. And for another, I hadn't wanted to. It wasn't so long ago that I made up stories about the animals outside my window, and it didn't seem right to kill them, fry them up, and swallow them down. Not when they could be attending tea parties or playing croquet while wearing velvet waistcoats and tam hats.

But by the afternoon, I was in a very desperate way. I couldn't think of how else to get food.

When you're hungry, you do things.

And so, I went to the shed to fetch the trap.

CHAPTER 9

THE SHED WAS MADE OUT OF PLANKS OF ROTTING BARN WOOD
fastened together with chicken wire. Inside the
shed was an old, rusted push mower, a cloth seed
sack, a wooden crate tied to a stick of oak, and a
ceramic garden gnome who went by the name of
Mr. Pitts.

I took the crate and the stick in one hand. Then
I stuffed the empty seed sack into the back pocket of
my jeans. Before heading out to the field, I wedged
Mr. Pitts under my arm.

"Careful with me now," Mr. Pitts seemed to say.
"I'm as old as the hills and in a delicate state—you
know, being made of clay."

"I know that, Mr. Pitts." I tightened my arm around his green overcoat.

If you ever spent a lot of time by yourself at the top of a mountain, with your very strange uncle gone or asleep and no one to talk to, after a while, just to have some company, you might strike up a conversation with whatever is around. Like a garden gnome, for example. You had to be real quiet and listen real close and use some imaginings, but if you did, sometimes they talked back.

Mr. Pitts had once belonged to the French painter Claude Monet, and for most of his life had lived in the Giverny Gardens, forty miles, as the crow flies, northwest of Paris. Or that's what we decided, anyway. Mr. Pitts and me.

Mr. Pitts was old. One of his eyes was set in a permanent winking position. He was missing his nose. Due to the cracks running through his head, he didn't know much about where he came from until I started reading to him, a couple of years ago, about Claude Monet and his gardens of water lilies in France. Then, lo and behold, after I finished reading the book for the second time, Mr. Pitts told me he wanted more than anything to have lived in those gardens. I said that he very well could have lived there, that anything was possible. And that was all it took. He believed.

He also wanted to believe he was a gift from Blanche, which was fine with me because the best parts in the Claude Monet book were the ones about Blanche. She was Claude Monet's favorite stepdaughter. They painted together, sometimes side by side, and she was the only one who could stand to be around him during his dark days and black moods.

His Blue Angel, that's what Claude Monet called Blanche.

You'd think that would make Mr. Pitts less of a grump, knowing where he was from and who he belonged to, but it very much did not.

"You've really gone and messed things up now," he told me.

"What did I do?"

"I don't know, but you must have done something."

"I haven't done anything," I said. "But things are a really big mess. I've got nothing to eat, Toot's gone, and yesterday I found out that curses are real. So . . ."

"Of course curses are real," said Mr. Pitts. "My

entire existence has been a curse. Just look at these cracks. Just look at my lack of nose. Do you know how hard it is to breathe without a nose?"

"You're made out of clay," I reminded him. "You can't breathe."

"Of course I can't breathe, dear girl. That is what I'm trying to tell you. Not without a nose."

He was starting to slip, so I hiked him up in my arm. His face turned into my armpit. Accidentally.

"Pure madness," said Mr. Pitts. "Not once did *le marquis,* my dear Monsieur Monet, ever leave me with such a view as this."

He was beginning to take this whole belonging-to-Monet thing a little too far, and I thought about telling him so. But I was having an awful day, so instead what I said was, "Maybe you'd like a close-up view of the gorge."

"Don't be cruel, Miss Grackle," he said. "It doesn't suit you. Now, why don't you just pay a visit to the town food pantry?"

"Because we've just been and can't go again for three weeks more," I answered. "Besides, with Toot gone, I've got no way to get there. It's too far to walk."

I shoved my heels into the backs of my too-small shoes as I flattened the tall devil's grass and rounded the shack. "If a better view is what you're after, I'll leave you by the garden." I set him down gently in the dirt, face up so that he could see the sun and sky. "That should put your complaints to bed," I said under my breath.

"Garden," muttered Mr. Pitts. "Miss Grackle, if you think this bare spot is a garden—"

Mr. Pitts made a string of remarks about the rectangle of clay dirt and weeds that I had so wanted to be a garden. To be full of sweet corn, bell peppers, string beans, and sugar snap peas. Watermelon, juicy cantaloupes, and honeydew melons. And tomatoes. Vines of plump tomatoes.

Toot loved tomatoes.

Toot. I felt a pang in my chest at what I'd said to her before she left. *Have fun with your mom.* I wished I could undo it. But things couldn't really be undone, could they?

I swung the trap as I walked the field just beyond the shed. The sun punished the back of my neck and bare shoulders. I found a small plot of clover near a wild chokecherry bush and dropped the crate in the middle. I propped up one side of the crate on a notch in the stick, like I'd seen Horace do, and carefully pushed the other end of the stick into the hard ground.

The crate tipped over. Again and again. I felt wronged. First by Charlie for taking all the food, then by Horace letting him, and now by the crate. I gave the crate a serious I'm-not-fooling look and said, "Stay put, you horrible thing."

I set the crate on the stick again. But the crate didn't even try. "How am I supposed to do this?"

"If I may, Miss Grackle," called Mr. Pitts from the garden. "You've got to make them each do the same amount of work. Don't let one get away with doing less than the other."

"Says the ceramic gnome lounging in the garden," I mumbled to myself. I brought the stick and the crate together, trying to give them each an equal load. It took four tries before I finally got them both in balance. "I did it," I said. Then louder, in the direction of Mr. Pitts. "I did it!"

"Of course, you did. Anybody could do it after I explained what needed to be done. Congratulations on being able to follow my expert instructions."

I ignored him. Then I took hold of the end of the rope and squatted behind the chokecherry bush.

It was early in the season, but I spotted a few cherries that were just beginning to get ripe. I pulled at a red one, which could have used another few days in the sun. It seemed to know that too, because it clung to its stem in an urgent way.

The first bite's bitterness made my cheeks pucker. I pulled off a few more and ate them fast without really tasting them. Then I took the seed sack from my pocket and filled it with the rest that were close to ripe, saving them for dinner. I tossed the bag of cherries a few feet behind me, out of eyeshot, so I wouldn't be tempted to gobble up the rest.

I wrapped the frayed end of the rope around my knuckle until my fingertip swelled and purpled. The view of the field from behind the chokecherry bush was as still and quiet as a painting. Except for a dragonfly, which darted into the scene and then away.

I waited.

I was good at waiting. I had lots of practice.

Waiting for summer to be over.

Waiting for my underwear to dry after a wash at the pump.

Waiting for the next trip to the food pantry.

Waiting for my parents to come back.

Waiting for life to get easier.

There was a trick to waiting, which had a lot to do with thinking about anything except the thing you were waiting for. The problem was, at the moment, I couldn't help but think of anything except food. I looked up at the sky to think of something else. Which would've worked fine if the clouds weren't in the shape of cheeseburgers.

The dragonfly returned. Then left again.

I closed my eyes. Sometimes seeing what wasn't there was worse than seeing nothing at all.

CHAPTER 10

THERE WAS A SUDDEN RUSH OF QUIET ON THE MOUNTAIN. THE leaves shook on their branches all at once, like they were shushing the creatures around them. Like the trees had a secret.

I listened close, hoping they might let me in on the secret. But whatever it was, the trees weren't in the mood for telling.

I got back to waiting. Not a single rabbit or squirrel in sight. And nothing to lure them into the trap with. After a while, I laid down my head in the hot grass. Sleep tugged at my eyelids.

It's hard to say how long I was asleep, maybe only a few minutes, maybe more, but I sat up suddenly with a feeling that I was being watched. My heart pounded in my chest. I looked around, expecting to see Horace and Charlie close by.

But the thing doing the watching wasn't Horace or Charlie. I relaxed a little when I spotted a raven next to the seed sack. "Oh, it's you," I said when I realized it was the same one-eyed bird that had given me the fortune. "Did you bring me something else? A sandwich, maybe?" I was really hoping for a sandwich.

He opened his beak wide, as if to show me it was empty. Then I told him, "Well, anyhow, I think I know why you brought me the fortune. You want help breaking the curse. You wanted my mama to do it ten years ago, but she wasn't able to for some reason, and now it's up to me. It's my destiny, like the fortune says. Is that right?"

The bird studied me for a second or two.

"But the thing is," I went on, "Charlie said that whatever's going to happen is going to happen in two days. And it was last night when he said that, so that means it will happen tomorrow when the moon comes. Tomorrow night. Which isn't much time when I don't even know what I'm supposed to be uncovering. I mean, I want to help you break the curse, but it would be a lot faster if you could just tell me, well, how."

The bird dove its head into the sack.

"Hey! I'm trying to talk to you." I clapped my hands, but the bird only hopped backward a few inches. It removed its head from the bag and showed off three plump chokecherries in its pointy black beak.

"No, no, those aren't for you!"

Then that bird looked at me with its one eye, as if to make sure I saw what would happen next. What happened next was this: The bird swallowed the chokecherries down in one gulp.

I'd never seen a bird gulp before, but that is what this bird did.

"Ah!" I yelled, waving my arms. "No!"

The bird didn't even try to get away.

I yelled again, stomping toward it. Nobody could say I was tall for being ten. I was tall-ish. But in any case, I was a whopping good deal taller than the raven, which was a very big bird but still a *bird*. My size should have frightened it. That was a rule of nature after all: big beats small.

The bird gave out a high-pitched knocking sound, and before I knew it, the feathery thief of a thing pinched one side of the sack in its beak and took off into the air.

I ran to the crate and grabbed the stick. I flung it at the bird, trying to knock the berries loose, but I missed the sack and the bird by a mile. I chased after it. The bird flew low. I leaped for the sack, but the bird held it just out of reach. I yelled for it to stop. To surrender! To give up the berries! Or else!

Another raven swooped down and flew alongside the first one, screeching and diving at my head.

My shoes pounded on the dry grass. I tried to keep up with the birds as they headed toward the tree line. But a cramp struck my side just below the ribs, and I slowed to a walk. The birds disappeared into the canopy of the forest before I even got to its edge.

I kept going. By the time I reached the trees, I had used up all my air, and my side felt like someone had stuck me with a meat fork. I lay down on the clump of pine needles by the base of a hemlock, swallowing mouthfuls of air. The pain in my side made me forget about how hungry I was and how mad. But that didn't last.

Low calls of ravens came from the top of the hemlock above me. Then their wings smacked the air like they were applauding their own cleverness. I looked up, but all I could see was green. Their calls echoed in the trees and funneled down to me, making my head dizzy with their screeching song. They were having a party up there, I could tell.

"Does everybody want to steal something from me? Go ahead! Because I don't have anything left!" I propped myself up on my elbows. "That was my dinner, you know!"

The birds went silent.

"I thought you wanted my help. You don't steal food from someone when you want them to help you." My voice was too heavy, too tired to be lifted above the trees. As if they would listen to reason, anyway.

Once again, the birds began chattering to one another, but quieter this time, and I swore they were laughing at me. They thought they were so good, way up there, with their feathers and their wings and their flying powers. The dinosaurs were their ancestors, though, and didn't the birds know what happened to them when they got a little too cozy roaming around the earth and eating up everything they pleased? Nothing like an asteroid barreling to Earth to teach them a lesson. Boom!

I looked up at the sky for asteroids, but it just wasn't my day.

The chokecherries were delicious.

What? The girl owed me.

Reciprocity. *Humans are supposed to know about this. I gave her the fortune, and she was supposed to give me something in return. One for one. And the chokecherries were right there.*

A bird needs sustenance.

At the top of the hemlock, one of the others from my flock passes me the tiny game token. It was the first thing I'd found on Smite Mountain. The first thing I put in my collection.

My memory of that day is imbued inside it for the girl to see.

This girl.

Of course, she's just like every other human I've encountered. Dim as a rusted nail.

And yet.

There's something else.

I fly down a bit closer so that I can look into her heart.

A bird's heart is much like a human's: four chambers, two atria, two ventricles.

The heart is a simple thing, really. Uncomplicated. Nothing like the brain, which makes an absolute mess of things.

The heart tells all. Everything I need to know is right inside.

It's how I knew that Magda could be trusted with our secret. It's why I thought she would help us break the curse.

All a bird needs to do, really, is wait for the human to be quiet. Still. Subdued.

Then it's as easy as looking into a window. Or a Dumpster.

The first heart I looked into was a fragile one. It belonged to a boy, long ago. He loved art. He loved color and light. I had never seen such light before.

I never could resist a shiny thing.

And yet.

There was something else too.

Fear.

A long shadow swallowing up the light. I visited him often and brought him trinkets, shiny things. I hoped the shadow would retreat.

I should have known what would happen. I should have known what the boy would do.

Below us, the girl is quiet now. No more yelling at us about stealing food.

Finally.

I get closer still.

What's this? Well now. A first.

It's no wonder the girl doesn't know what she must do.

Her heart is shuttered. Closed. Walled off.

Like a Dumpster with its lid down.

CHAPTER 11

ALL AT ONCE, THE BIRDS LEFT THE HEMLOCK. THEY DOVE STRAIGHT at me and then took off down the mountain. They were gone, just like that.

"Where are you going? Come back!" I yelled after them.

I thought of Mr. Desmond's question again. *If a tree falls in the forest, and nobody is around to hear it, does it make a sound?* I yelled as loud as I could for the birds to come back, but they just kept on flying as if they couldn't hear me.

I wanted to believe I still made sounds.

Toot said I had the makings of a luminary. Someone who could look straight into darkness and see a way through when nobody else could.

Then, inside my pocket, I felt the heartbeat from the fortune thumping. And I thought of another question: *If destiny was calling, would a luminary answer that call?*

That answer was easy.

Yes, yes, yes.

A luminary would always answer the call of destiny. So I got myself up and went after the birds.

It was easier to catch up with them than I would've thought. The birds were noisy, constantly calling to one another as they flew. There must be a great deal of navigational conversation required to keep a flock together: "Everyone, to the air! Turn right at that tree with the squirrel's nest, now left at that diseased holly bush. Don't lollygag about! Stay together! Oh look, a hungry young girl with berries. Descend!"

I followed them to Whistling Creek but then lost them. I left the shade of the hemlocks and went into the clearing where the creek divided the mountain in half. The sun beat down, and I jumped straight into the water.

The creek bed was low, with only a few inches of water above the rocks. I sat down in the middle of it, letting the cool water seep through my jeans and spill over my legs. I cupped some water into my hands, drank it, and cupped some more.

Then I lay back in the water and closed my eyes. I imagined that I was part of the creek. That I could make myself small and become a crayfish, riding along for miles and miles until I finally came to the sea.

Creeks were never stuck in one place.

Creeks were never searching.

Creeks were never hungry.

I dug my fingers into the bottom of the creek bed and scooped up a handful of muck. Then I opened my eyes to see what I had caught. Pebbles and mud mostly, but also a rusted bottle cap. I dunked the pebbles and the bottle cap back into the creek to rinse them, then I stuffed the bottle cap in my pocket and put the pebbles, just the smooth ones, inside my cheek. The rest went back into the water.

The pebbles were sugared candy. That's what I imagined as I moved them from one cheek to the other. After a while, they filled me up. This was a trick

I had learned a few years before, and it worked most of the time. Who knows why sucking on stones fooled my stomach, but it did.

When the sun dipped below the treetops, the ravens returned. They came out from the forest edge and swooped above me. One still had the seed sack in its beak, the rotten thief. I spit the stones back into the water and climbed out of the creek.

Wringing the water from my jeans and shirt, I watched as the birds headed south toward the valley. I started after them but stopped. It would be dark soon. *Am I really going to chase these birds all over the mountain in the dark for a few cherries?*

I turned away.

I didn't get far before the birds circled back and flew in front of me.

The one-eyed raven was so close, I thought it might peck out my eyeballs. I covered my head with an arm and pointed down the mountain with the other. "Murderation! Gypsum is that way. I'm sure there's someone down there who wouldn't mind sharing some food."

The bird made croaking sounds at me. *Rrack, rrack, rrack.*

I lowered my arm. "What do you want?"

It dove at me from behind, and its wingtips brushed against my shoulder.

I ducked and squatted in the grass. "You know, if you're going to keep acting this way, I'm not sure why I should help you break the curse."

The bird circled around me again and then let something go from its talons.

Whatever it was bounced once on the ground in front of me. On my hands and knees, I sifted through the tall grass until I found it. This time it wasn't a fortune; it was a toy car, made out of metal and smaller than my thumb.

I closed my hand over the car and was about to put it in my pocket when the same jolt of electricity that I had felt before with the fortune shot through my hand, up my arm, and went straight as an arrow to my chest. Like before, everything in front of me—the grass, my hand holding the tiny car—blurred and then faded away. Soon they were replaced by the wide porch of a farmhouse. The trees surrounding the house were thick with spring blossoms. As they came into focus, I saw a young boy setting up a game of Monopoly on the porch.

"I don't have all day!" yelled the boy, who looked to be about twelve or thirteen. He was sorting the Monopoly money into tidy piles.

"Keep your pants on, Horace! I said I was coming," a girl's voice called from inside a root cellar near the house. "And I'm the car."

Horace? I stared at him and climbed the steps of the porch to get a closer look. His face was smooth and round, and so full. Without all of the angles and deep lines and patchy whiskers and coating of dirt. One of his eyes was swollen and bruised. "No way," Horace called back. "I'm always the car."

A shadow flitted across the porch. Horace didn't seem to notice. But I did. Six ravens flew low near the porch and came to rest in a tall pine next to the house.

Horace took the metal game token from the box and set it on the porch railing. The tiny car was silver and shiny and reflected the sun. Horace made engine-revving noises as he raced the car along the rail. *Vrooor-vrooor-bubb-bubb-vroooooor.*

As he rounded the corner of the porch, he stopped. A raven sat there waiting, curious. At the sight of the shiny car, the bird flew at it. Horace swiped it away from the bird's snapping beak and held on to the token, tight in his fist.

Boy and bird, the two stood there in the afternoon sun, staring at each other.

Slowly, Horace reached out his empty hand to the raven. Cautiously, and very, very slowly, the bird leaned its neck closer to the boy. When he touched the raven's feathers with his knuckles, Horace broke into a wide smile.

I'd never seen anything like it land on his face before.

Then he pulled a small notebook and a charcoal pencil from his back pocket and began to draw the bird. His pencil moved so fast across the page, it was like it knew exactly what to do.

"Ready to lose?" said a girl behind us. She was carrying a jar of something that looked like pears.

There she was. *Magda. My mama.* She was a lot younger in this memory than the one from the fortune. She looked like maybe she was sixteen. She passed right by me, and I reached out to touch her, but my hand went right through her. *You aren't there, remember,* I told myself. *She can't see you.*

The raven startled at the sight of her and flew away.

"In a second." Horace stuffed the notebook and pencil back into his pocket. Then he leaned on the railing and searched the sky for the bird.

"What are you looking at?" asked Magda. She opened the jar and reached inside. She pulled out a pear dripping with syrup and ate it.

"Nothing," he said. "Come on."

I followed them both back to the other side of the porch where the Monopoly game was set up.

Magda wiped her syrupy hand on her pants. Then she grabbed Horace's chin and lifted. "How's your eye?"

Horace wriggled free. "It's nothing." He touched the purple bruise.

"That slimy pig Charlie Mullet," she said. "He's no good. Why do you hang around with him?"

Horace shook his head and shrugged.

"What did Pa say?" asked Magda.

Horace squeezed the metal car tighter in his fist. "He said that Charlie Mullet knows how to land a punch."

"Well then." She sighed. "I found a lantern and some art books in the root cellar. Were you hiding from Pa again?"

"Maybe," he said, looking away.

She patted him on his shoulder. "Don't fret about your eye. It's a nice shade of purple. Maybe it'll inspire your next painting."

Horace smiled again. "Maybe so."

"Junior!" said a man as he came around the side of the house. His coveralls were streaked with grease, and he was gripping an old steering wheel in one hand and a rifle in the other.

Horace's smile disappeared. The wind shifted direction.

"Yes, Pa?" Horace let the car fall from his hand onto the game board. It landed on Chance.

"Look here now." Pa held out the rifle to him. "This was my grandpappy's twenty-two." He turned the gun over, admiring it. "Got it cleaned all up and working like a champ."

Horace looked from the gun to his father. He nodded.

"Well?" said Pa. "What do you say?"

"You did a good job," said Horace. He took a step closer to get a better look at the swirling grain of the wood, like he was appraising a work of art. "Deep raw umber. Beautiful color."

His father flared his nostrils and squared his jaw. "I'm giving it to you, boy," he said.

"Oh."

Pa stared at Horace. "Don't you know what this means? You can come hunting with me and the guys now that you've got your own gun," he said. "I'd think you might show a little appreciation."

Horace forced another nod. "Yes, sir. Thank you."

The sound of two gunshots rang out from somewhere on the mountain. Horace jumped, and so did I.

"That's probably Leroy Mullet and his boy Charlie shootin' targets," said Pa. "He says that Charlie is some good shot."

Horace looked down at the game board. He said nothing.

Pa stood there for a moment, wiped his forehead on his shirtsleeve, and then walked away. "Some good shot," he said again under his breath.

"Why didn't you tell him?" asked Magda when Pa was gone. "Why didn't you just say you don't want to go hunting?"

Horace shook his head.

Magda dealt out the Monopoly money. "You'd think Pa would soon realize that no matter how hard he tries, you're never going to be like him."

"Shut up," he said.

Magda stopped and looked at him. "Aw, come on, Horace. Now you know I didn't mean . . ."

Horace didn't let her finish. He picked up the metal car from the board. Then he threw it as hard as he could into the cornfield next to the house.

When the memory was over, the cornfield blurred.

As it faded away, I was back in the tall grass next to

the one-eyed raven. I propped myself up on my elbows and looked at the bird. "That was my uncle, Horace. He was an artist?" *So the book about the painter Claude Monet—it belonged to Horace.*

The ravens began making croaking calls.

"I don't speak bird."

Suddenly, the one-eyed bird latched onto my front pants pocket with its beak. Its talons clung to the seam of my jeans. "Ow!" I yelled, swatting him away. "Get off!" Somehow the bird managed to get its beak inside my pocket and grab the bottle cap I'd found in the creek. Then the bird pushed off me and took flight.

I got to my feet. The rest of the flock was in the air, flying away from me, just a few feet and then back again. Their low, croaking calls quickly changed to high-pitched screeches. "I don't know what you want," I told them. They gathered behind me, all five of them, flying close. I took a few steps forward. They moved ahead of me and then doubled back behind me when I stopped. I turned to face them. "Okay. You want me to follow you? Is that it?"

Their answer must have been yes because they flew on past me down the mountain, keeping low to the ground like they wanted to make it easy for me to keep up. And I thought, *Hey, maybe I can speak bird, after all.*

CHAPTER 12

I HAD NEVER BEEN THIS FAR EAST PAST THE CREEK. THE AIR WAS different here. It made the hair prickle on the back of my neck.

The mountain on this side of Whistling Creek was steep. Careful with my footing, I stayed right close to the creek so that I could find my way back up. The creek flowed through a clearing with switchgrass that came up to my waist. I stepped slowly so I wouldn't surprise a snake, but more so a snake wouldn't surprise *me*.

The stiff grass clawed at my pants, even stuck me through the wet denim, which I didn't much appreciate.

The ravens took wide circles around me until I caught up with them.

Hollow. That was the only word I could think of to describe the feeling of this place. Like there was ancient life here at one time, before it was scooped out and thrown away, like the insides of somebody's Halloween pumpkin.

I hurried my steps through the forest, dodging the tall pines. The creek too seemed to be in a big rush as it bumped into rocks, fizzing and spraying into the air.

Finally, I came to the valley where the mountain smoothed into a green meadow and where Whistling Creek got about twenty feet wide. The ravens took cover in the treetops.

"What now?" I asked them. I'd followed the birds all this way. *For what?*

Then something across the meadow caught my eye: a silver camper and a pickup truck.

I crouched behind a young cypress and watched. A man on his knees was staring into a hole in the ground. Beside him were two shovels leaning against a pile of dirt nearly as tall as me. A wide frame of wood with a mesh screen was next to the pile. There were other holes too. At least eight more that I could see. "What is this about?" I whispered. I kept my eyes on the man as he swept something on the side of the hole with a small brush.

He took off his wide-brimmed hat and wiped his forehead with his shirtsleeve. What little hair he had on his head, he made up for on his face. A thick gray beard hid his chin and cheeks and barely left enough space for his glasses. I craned my neck around the tree to see what might be in that hole, and as I did, the man called out, "I know what you're doing!"

A bird's screech echoed off the trees. I froze. Even *I* didn't know what I was doing. So what did the man think *he* knew? I tried to make myself as small as I could. *A baby mouse, a walnut, a kernel of corn, a grain of wheat, a piece of dirt, a speck of dust. A baby mouse, a walnut, a kernel of corn . . .*

I wondered if I could make a run for it, if I could make it back up the mountain to my woods before he caught me and put me into one of his holes. The man didn't look like he would be very fast, but I didn't put much stock into how things looked. I'd read about some species of spiders that disguised themselves as ants by waving their front legs near their heads like antennae, so they could fool the ants and then eat them.

I didn't want to be eaten.

"I could use some help, you know," the man called out.

I peered around the tree again. The man was looking at something in his hand. He blew on it and rubbed it with his shirtsleeve. Then he held it up above him, to catch the last of the day's sun. A marble? A chunk of gold? Whatever it was, it was too small to see from here. The man shook his head and dropped the thing back into the hole.

Just then, a boy came out of the camper. He had reddish-brown hair that stood up all over, straight and even, like mowed grass. And he was short, at least a foot shorter than me, not counting the hair.

The boy limped. Even so, he seemed to take his time getting to the man.

When the boy finally got to the dirt pile, the man pointed at the framed screen. They talked, or the man did at least. I could hear bits and pieces, words like *agreement* and *gave us your word* and *expect of you*. They were the kind of words that tied your hands when you heard them. The boy looked at the ground the whole time, like he was hoping it would open up and swallow him whole. Then, when the man was done talking, and the ground hadn't done any swallowing, the boy turned around and went back inside the camper.

The man's shoulders slumped, and a few minutes later he went after the boy. On the way, he kicked the framed screen against the dirt pile. Dust plumed into the air.

I leaned my back against the bark of the cypress. I kept wondering about the holes. So many holes.

That Izzy lady at the food pantry said that people on the mountain had disappeared. Did this man and boy—and these holes—have something to do with it? Is that why the ravens led me down here?

My stomach grumbled, and I told it to be quiet.

It didn't listen.

I could just go, I thought. *Leave now and get back to my rock shelter.*

But why did the ravens lead me here? Is there something in the holes they wanted me to see?

I wanted to see. Just see what was in them.

The camper door was shut. The blinds were pulled closed. There was a shadow behind one of the windows. Then two. I knew I couldn't wait forever. My stomach churned and grumbled again. It was on the verge of a tantrum. So as fast as I could, I ran to the nearest hole. It was about four feet deep and as wide as a refrigerator. *Murderation! It's empty and big enough to fit a body.* A cold tingle went through me.

I ran to the other holes. They were smaller but empty too.

Nothing but dirt inside.

The shadows in the camper moved past the window, so I took off to the truck for some cover. I crouched down by the back tire and waited. My heart was thundering up a storm in my ears.

I kept my eyes on the camper door, but nobody came out. After a while, my legs started to ache, and I told myself that now was the time to go. Now, before the man and the boy came back out again and saw me. Now, before they put me into one of their holes.

But now came and went. I wiped the sweat from my face with my T-shirt. I couldn't make myself move.

Now, I told myself again.

Now.

Come on. Now.

My legs finally listened, and they got me standing at least. That's when I saw the tote bags. They were lined up beneath the truck's rear window. A bag of potato chips was sticking out of one.

I saw the potato chips with my eyes. But somehow my stomach saw them too, because the next thing I knew, I was hoisting one leg up on the truck's gate and then the other. Those chips were calling to me. "Cutie Grackle's stomach," the chips seemed to say, "we are delicious. And by the way, you should see what else is in these bags."

It's not every day when potato chips call to you.

The chips were right too, because the tote bags were chock-full of groceries, and I wondered if maybe the monster on the mug that Horace broke knew a thing or two. Maybe good things did happen, once in a while.

Then my stomach. It answered the potato chips' call. With such a noise. Not a quiet gurgle or even a polite rumble.

Like a mountain lion being torn apart by a bear. *Blurrrrghhhhhpubbbbreeeeer!!!!!*

And it was loud.

Very, very loud.

I stared at the camper door, embarrassed at the prospect of having digestive problems that sounded like an animal attack, and waited for the man and the boy to burst out, guns ablazing.

They didn't come.

Quickly, I pulled out the bag of potato chips, along with the biggest jar of fruit jam I had ever seen, a package of circus peanuts, and a six-pack of root beer that was tucked all the way at the bottom under a roll of toilet paper.

With my arms full, I stopped. I had never, not even once, taken anything that belonged to someone else. Even the food I took from the cafeteria at school came from the trash can, not from other kids' trays. Now, in front of me, there seemed to be some line that was drawn, and if I crossed it, things would change. *I* would change.

I put down the root beer. I told myself that I would not ever be a thief like Charlie. But then my stomach, in a symphony of animal attacks, seemed to be fighting my brain for control of the situation.

It was sending all sorts of chemical messengers back and forth.

Stomach: FEED ME! NOW!

Brain: Settle down. We'll figure something out.

Stomach: MUST HAVE FOOD!

Brain: Stealing is wrong. We could go to jail. And jail is not a suitable place for us.

Stomach: THERE IS FOOD IN JAIL!

Brain: Let me think.

Stomach: IF YOU DON'T FEED ME SOON, YOU WILL BE SORRY.

Brain: If she steals from them, we will feel ashamed, and we will all be sorry. Unless, of course, she leaves a note of explanation. Oh yes, a note of explanation could make all the difference.

Stomach: NOW YOU'RE THINKING!

I spotted a backpack at the end of the line of tote bags. I put down the food and unzipped the main compartment and felt around, hoping for something to write on and with. My fingers landed on a notebook and pen. I already knew what my note would say:

Dear man and boy, diggers of holes:

I took some of your food.

Which I feel very, very, very sorry about.
But when you're hungry, you do things.

—Me

I didn't have a chance to write a single word, though, because suddenly, the ravens began calling to one another in a high-pitched panic. *Rrack-rrack-rrack.*

They took off into the air. I shoved the notebook, potato chips, and circus peanuts into the backpack. But as I picked up the giant jar of jam, it slipped from my fingers.

It was like slow motion, watching it fall. I closed one eye. Whatever was going to happen, it was going to be too awful to see with both eyes.

The jar hit the metal floor of the truck bed, and there was a loud crash followed by a cracking of glass. Strawberry jam splattered everywhere.

The door of the camper flew open just as my feet hit the ground. I swung the backpack with the food over my shoulders and took off across the meadow and into the woods. I followed the creek back to my forest and didn't stop until I got to my rock shelter, where I disappeared inside.

CHAPTER
13

THE FIRST HANDFULS OF SOUR CREAM AND ONION POTATO CHIPS tasted like victory. But as I got deeper into the bag, they began to taste bitter, like someone else's dirty socks. I tried to wash away the taste with a circus peanut and the strawberry jam that had splattered onto my jeans, but even that tasted wrong. (I'd never had a circus peanut before, and I never will again because it was like eating a Styrofoam banana.)

My stomach seemed as happy as a pig in mud, though, and didn't even bother me once.

I propped myself up against the cold rock wall inside the shelter and closed my eyes. The paper fortune and metal car felt heavy in my pocket.

The holes were empty, so what did the birds want me to do? Or did they know about the food there? Is that what they wanted me to find? My head was chock-full of questions. It felt like there were dandelion seeds blowing around inside my skull, trying to take root. I didn't know anything more than before I went down there. Except this: I wasn't alone on the mountain.

I took out my flashlight from the burlap sack and pointed it at the backpack. Maybe I could find out something about the man and the boy and what they're doing. The zipper pull had a piece of braided twine hanging from it, and on the end of the twine was a metal pendant in the shape of an anchor. It had specks of rust on it and was worn smooth.

I pulled the twine to unzip the backpack, and I emptied it into my lap. A leather notebook, a compass on a key ring, and a pack of spearmint gum fell out. Also, a small box of tissues. The kind with lotion inside.

Even when they had things like tissues and toilet paper at the No Hunger Food Pantry, which wasn't very often, they never had the kind with lotion. I pulled out a single tissue from the pack and rubbed

it in circles along my cheek. If my mama ever rubbed her thumb along my face, I wondered, *Did it feel like this? Were her hands this soft? Was this what it felt like to be loved?*

The potato chips made me thirsty, and I wished I had taken the root beer instead of the circus peanuts. I stuffed a stick of gum into my mouth and chewed and chewed, swallowing all the spearmint flavor in big gulps.

Then I opened the notebook.

A black ink pen was tucked between pages, hanging from a twisted cord. On the inside cover was written in thick block letters: THIS CHRONICLE IS THE PROPERTY OF GALEN PODARSKI.

"What's a chronicle?" I said.

And underneath that: NOTICE: Anyone other than Galen Podarski who makes the ~~unwise~~ stupid decision to turn the page and go any further will be cursed. Do you understand? Painfully and for eternity. Like, your life will be completely messed up.

"Oh," I said, understanding. "It's a diary."

I flipped to the first page, past the warning. "You will be cursed," I repeated out loud.

Seems like there's a lot of that going around.

Then I saw the list.

1. Chandra Bahadur Dangi, a farmer from Nepal, is the shortest living person in the world. He is 21.5 inches tall. (Which is ~~28.5~~ 27.5 inches shorter than me.)

2. An atom is the smallest unit of ordinary matter that retains all the properties of a chemical element. A single atom is about one hundred thousand times thinner than a strand of human hair. Splitting a certain kind of atom can cause a chain reaction (and other science-y stuff I don't really understand). The main point: There is enough energy in a tiny atom that, when split, it can create a HUGE explosion. KAPOW!

There were eight entries on the first page, and the list kept going, page after page.

13. Patu digua is the smallest known species of spiders. They live in Colombia and are the size of a period. Seriously, a dot. Like this one right here: .

25. The butterfly effect. Coined by a man named Edward Lorenz. It's the idea that something as small as a butterfly

could influence world events. A butterfly flapping its wings in New Mexico, for example, can cause a hurricane in China. If that butterfly had not flapped its wings in that exact moment in time and at that exact location, the hurricane would not have happened.

Could that be true? Could a butterfly really cause a hurricane halfway around the world?

I closed the diary and laid it on the ground beside me. Then I picked up the compass and held it under the flashlight, watching the needle find north. Even when I shook it or turned it upside down, the needle knew where it belonged.

Then I snapped the bird disk onto the flashlight and pointed it at the wall of the rock shelter. The circle of light that I pretended was the moon still had hold of the bird. I wondered if it would ever let the bird go free.

By this time, the gum had lost all its flavor and green color and now tasted like rain boots, so I stuck it to the wall until morning. I stretched out on the dirt floor and switched off my flashlight.

The crickets were singing their nighttime song.

The katydids were calling to someone named Katy, asking if she did or if she didn't.

In the dark, holding tight to the tissue, I closed my eyes and listened.

CHAPTER 14

THIS TIME, IT WAS THE SUN, AND NOT MY STOMACH, THAT WOKE me. It crawled into my rock shelter and peered at me with irritating determination until I finally gave in and opened my eyes.

The air was hot and sticky.

My mouth was dry. My tongue felt like it had put on a fur coat. And I had a pain the size of Texas in my head.

I sat up and found the pack of gum on the dirt floor. I plucked out a new piece. It looked like a present, all wrapped up in shiny silver foil.

But the thing was, it wasn't a present. I had stolen it.

All of a sudden, a heavy, sick feeling came over me.

Did Charlie and Horace feel this way after they took all the food? Am I the same as them?

No. That's what I told myself. *No, no, no.* I wasn't like them. To prove it, I would make it right. I couldn't give the boy and the man back what I took, not all of it, anyway, but I would give them something in return. I slid the new piece of gum back into its pack. Then I pulled last night's hard, gray wad of chewed gum from the rock wall and stuck it back into my mouth.

I looked around inside the rock shelter to take stock of everything I had. On the floor: the diary/ chronicle (theirs), tissues (theirs), magic lantern (mine), spearmint gum (theirs), half-eaten bag of sour cream and onion potato chips (theirs), and nearly full bag of circus peanuts (yuck, theirs). In my mouth: wad of chewed gum (mine now, used to be theirs). In my pocket: the fortune (mine) and the Monopoly car (mine now, used to belong to the ravens, and before that, Horace).

There wasn't much.

That's when I remembered the compass. I scanned the dirt floor for it and checked the backpack a couple of times, but it wasn't anywhere.

Then I saw something on the ground at the entrance to the shelter. It was a thin metal tube, rusted and tapered at one end. It made me wonder: *Did the ravens steal the compass and bring me this while I was sleeping?*

I crawled out of the rock shelter and looked for the ravens in the nearby hemlocks. But the trees and the tiny bits of blue sky carved out between them were birdless.

A butterfly flitted past me. It seemed to say, "What on Earth are you waiting for?"

I took a deep breath and steadied myself. Then I picked up the metal tube and squeezed it in my hand. Right away, a jolt of electricity went straight to my heart. Then everything in front of me faded away. And I faded away with it.

In a moment, I was back at the farmhouse.

It was nighttime. There was a full moon hanging high above. It looked like an egg.

There was a boy too. He came out of the root cellar and stopped to look up at the moon. He had a raven on his shoulder and a painting stuffed under his arm.

The boy was Horace.

I stepped closer to him and noticed that the purple bruise under his eye from Charlie's punch had faded

to yellow. I knew he couldn't see me, because I wasn't really there. I was just inside a memory, watching, but still. I wanted to make sure. "Horace?" I said. "You can't hear me, right?"

Horace didn't say anything. He untucked the painting from his arm and looked it over. It was a picture of an old car and a man who looked a lot like Horace's father standing beside it. It looked like something Claude Monet might've painted and thought was good enough to not set on fire. Horace adjusted the ribbon that was tied around the canvas. Then he climbed the wooden steps to the front porch.

I could hear arguing inside.

Horace heard it too. He stopped at the front door.

"Do you know the ribbing I get from Barclay and Elmer and the other fellas about him?" It was Horace's father. "He quit Little League after one season. No interest in the coal mine. Found him hiding out in the root cellar the other day, reading about art and painting pictures and other worthless nonsense. Shoot, gave him a huntin' rifle, and he won't even touch it. If my father gave me something like that, you bet I'd have been begging him to take me out."

110

"He may have your name," said Horace's mother, "but he's not you."

His father scoffed. "You got that right."

Horace stood there, listening, and his face turned pale. The raven on his shoulder puffed out its chest.

"He's young and—"

"Leroy Mullet's boy Charlie is the same age," said his pa, "and he's been hunting deer with Leroy since he could walk. Leroy was telling me that just last month, Charlie shot a coyote, a bunch of skunks, a possum, and a weasel."

"You want Horace to be more like Charlie?" Horace's mother said. "Let me tell you something, Charlie Mullet is no sweepstakes prize."

"Well, from where I'm standing, he's more of a prize than—"

"Don't you say that," said his mother. "He's our son."

"Yours, maybe," said his father. "That boy, shoot, he's no son of mine."

Horace sucked in a shallow breath. Then he shook the raven from his shoulder and dropped the painting. He threw open the front door.

I followed.

"Is that you, Junior?" Horace's mother called from the kitchen. "Junior?"

Horace didn't answer. He went to his room and grabbed a knapsack off his bed. The walls of his room were just about completely covered with paintings done on drawing paper. There were lots of the mountain, in every season, and there were wispy meadows too and all kinds of trees. Horace had even painted the raven a couple of times. All in the style of Claude Monet and the Impressionists—blurry and dreamy with lots of light and shadow.

And above his dresser, there was a painting of Magda. She was sitting in a field of flowers. It was so beautiful, I couldn't look away.

Until Horace started ripping it down. He tore all his paintings, crumpled them into balls, and stuffed them into his knapsack like they were trash. Paintbrushes too. Then he grabbed his flashlight from on top of his dresser.

"What are you doing?" said Magda, who stood in the doorway to his room.

I startled at the sound of my mama's voice.

"I'm good for nothing." Horace wiped his eyes on his shirtsleeve. "Pa said so."

Magda came into his room and closed the door behind her. "You're different from him, that's all," she told him. "Pa doesn't understand different."

Horace grabbed his rifle that was propped up next to his dresser.

That's when I noticed the raven, sitting on the windowsill, watching.

"What are you fixin' to do?" Magda said.

"If he wants me to be like Charlie," said Horace, sniffing. "Then I'll show him Charlie." He climbed out his bedroom window and onto the porch. The raven flew off.

"Horace, don't," Magda called after him. "Please. Please come back."

Outside, in the light of the full moon, Horace slung the knapsack over his shoulder and walked across the field to the burn barrel. I followed him.

Then I watched as Horace threw his paintings into the rusted barrel. He pulled out his wooden paintbrushes from his knapsack and broke them over his knee. A few pieces missed the barrel, but he left them on the ground where they fell. He took off up the mountain.

In the dirt, a metal tube that bound the bristles to the handle glinted in the moonlight. *Is this the same metal tube the birds left me?* A raven swooped down in front of me then and snatched the tube that was on the ground, and I knew it was.

The raven disappeared into the night sky. I followed Horace all the way up the mountain. He was breathing heavy, and it sounded thick and wet like he was crying, but he kept on going, shifting the strap of his rifle from one shoulder to the other, until he finally stopped near an outcropping of boulders. Then he fell to his knees in the grass. He laid down the flashlight beside him. "You want me to be like you?" he said, sliding the butt of the rifle into the pocket of his shoulder. "That will make you proud?"

The raven came then. It was hard to see it in the dark. But I saw it fly close to Horace.

Horace asked the question again. "This is the kind of son you want, right?" He took aim, pointing the rifle into the dark. At the raven.

Didn't Horace see the raven there?

Screeches came from other birds in a tree close by. Short bursts that sounded like an alarm. Then a click from inside the rifle, and Horace answered himself. "Right."

In the quiet that followed, the raven spoke. "Right," the bird said. Its voice was like an old man's who had a sore throat.

Horace flinched at the voice in the dark. Then came the crack of the rifle. It sounded as though the sky had split open. Horace was knocked onto his back. The rifle fell.

I saw the bird before Horace did. I saw what he had done to the poor raven's eye.

Moments later, Horace righted himself and picked up his flashlight. When he saw what he had done, he yelled. He scrambled to his feet. Grabbed the rifle. And ran for home.

CHAPTER 15

WHEN THE MEMORY WAS OVER, I PUSHED THE METAL TUBE DEEP into my pocket and pulled out my hand as fast as I could.

The forest was spinning. Or maybe I was; I couldn't tell. The strange flutter inside me had returned, and my head throbbed. I put my hand on the middle of my chest and felt my heart jumping. Like there were too many beats going at once. *Is something happening to my heart?*

I sat down in the grass.

In case the one-eyed raven was out there, listening, I looked up into the sky and said, "That was you? Horace did that to your eye?"

I closed my eyes tight until the spinning stopped. When I opened them, the one-eyed bird was standing in the tall grass in front of me.

"Does it have something to do with the curse?" I asked.

The bird looked at me with his one eye. He wasn't giving anything away.

"Look, from what Charlie and Horace said about the curse, something's supposed to happen tonight. But the thing is, I don't know what exactly. There was an old lady at the food pantry who said people started disappearing on this mountain years ago. If I can't break the curse in time, is that what's going to happen? Will Horace and Charlie disappear?"

Nothing.

"I heard you speak before, in the memory. You said, 'Right.' You said it to Horace. It would be a whole lot easier to help you if you would talk to me."

The raven bobbed its head. Then the bird stretched out a wing and started running feathers through its beak. One by one.

"I'll wait," I said, watching. The bird didn't seem to mind me staring.

Toot was always telling me not to stare at people the same way I stared at the paintings in the Claude Monet book. Which I knew, but sometimes forgot, and most of the time I couldn't help. I stared at paintings so I could know everything about them: the brushstrokes, the colors, the feelings. But this bird wasn't a person, and as far as I could tell, it didn't seem bothered.

The longer I watched, the more I noticed. Like how the morning sun on his feathers made them look more blue than black. Midnight blue. Claude Monet might've wanted to paint such a fine-looking scene. Except he probably would've used ivory black instead because he only ever used nine colors in his paintings and midnight blue wasn't one of them.

But anyhow, I could imagine the way the bird might look if Claude Monet painted it. Colorful but blurry, like you were looking at it through squinty eyes. Or seeing it in a dream. Like you were noticing the impression of the bird but not the bird itself. The painting would probably be called something like *Bird in Woods* because even though Mr. Monet's paintings were masterpieces, he stunk at giving them names. *Woman with a Parasol* was one. *The Lunch* was another. *The Water-Lily Pond.* I mean, that was the best he could do?

I started thinking of what I would call the painting of this bird, if there was one. *The Magical, Mysterious One-Eyed Raven of Smite Mountain, Desperate to Right the Wrongs of the World.*

It was a bit long, but still, at least it told you something.

When the raven finally finished cleaning its feathers, I said, "Well? Are you going to tell me something or not?"

Nothing happened.

"I guess that's a not," I said. "You must be a little leery of people after what happened to your eye. But don't worry, I won't hurt you." Then I reached out to the raven, just as Horace had done in the memory from the Monopoly car. But the bird backed away from me. "It's okay," I said, opening my hand, inching closer. "I promise."

The bird flew behind me to the top of my rock shelter.

"Well, fine," I said, turning to face him. "Don't tell me, then. But if you're going to keep showing up like this, I think I should know what to call you. Toot—she's my friend—she says that things with names are easier to relate to, so let me see." The one-eyed bird watched me while I thought of one. "How about Claude? For Mr. Claude Monet. He was a famous French painter. But maybe you already know that?"

If birds knew how to put memories inside small objects, maybe they knew a lot of other things.

I cleared my throat. "The Prince of Light, he was called. The Father of Impressionism."

He was also called "old lunatic," "poor old crustacean," and "frightful old hedgehog." But I decided not to mention that.

"'He who came to find upon the waves, among the reflections of sky and water, the figure of life's eternal dream,'" I said, reciting from a part of the Monet book I knew by heart. "That's what they wrote about him when he died. I don't know what it means exactly, but it has a nice sound, don't you think?"

The bird pecked at its rear end.

"All right, then." I went on anyway. "For a good part of his life, Mr. Monet could only see out of one eye too."

The bird stopped pecking and looked at me. I wondered if it was waiting for me to do something ceremonial to mark the occasion. So I snapped off a thin branch of a hemlock, waved it in a circle around my head, and said, "I now pronounce you Claude, Bird of the Highest Order." Then I laid the branch by his feet.

That must've done the trick, because then Claude puffed up the feathers around his head, lifted his bill, and spread his shoulders. He bowed and stretched his wings and tail. Then he made a noise that sounded like a sigh.

I stuck out my arms and bowed in return.

I am now Claude, Bird of the Highest Order.

I don't know what that means.

But I kind of like it.

Of course, I've had other names. Ravens can have a hundred names over a lifetime. When I was born, my parents called me Lune. After they left me, I called myself Libero. And then, for a short time, after I lost my eye, I was called Oculus.

Most recently, I went by Briller. Because the more brilliant the object, the more desirable it is to me. The world is full of shiny objects to find.

On this day, though, I'm not looking for shiny things. My attention is elsewhere.

The map, in particular. Hasn't she found it?

The boy put it in his backpack. I saw him yesterday after he discovered it. That was the entire point of leading the girl to his campsite. To retrieve his backpack, find the map, and break the curse.

Bim, bam, boom. Simple. Even for a human.

The girl has two eyes and quite a large brain. How difficult is it to locate a piece of paper inside a backpack?

Truly.

This girl.

She wants me to speak to her. To tell her what needs to be done.

Impossible.

Imitating human sound is forbidden and comes at a price. I did it once, and it cost me my eye.

I can afford to pay no more. The magic I've spent to show her my memories has already begun to take its toll.

The memories should be enough to open her heart! To make her understand!

And yet.

Perhaps I've made an error in judgment about this girl.

She hides behind trees or inside rock shelters. She talks to a ceramic garden gnome. She can't even trap a varmint.

If only I could see inside her heart.

When the girl is quiet, and I can hear her heart thrumming, I try to look again.

Shuttered, it remains.

I have only one more object from my collection that is imbued with a memory. One more chance to make her understand.

There were others. A silver button in the shape of an anchor. A gold rose pendant.

But they have been lost over the years.

So much has been lost.

Claude poked his head out of the backpack.

I squatted down and held out a circus peanut. "I think these are gross, but maybe you'll like them."

Claude hopped out of the backpack and came over to me. He took the circus peanut out of my fingers lickety-split and swallowed it whole. "Oh, so you like Styrofoam bananas, then. Good to know."

He looked at me. I understood that kind of look. He wanted another. This time I tossed a peanut into the air to see if he'd catch it. The circus peanut hit him on the head and bounced on the ground. I didn't know that birds could look annoyed, but that was how this bird looked at me. "Oh sorry," I said. "You don't catch." I handed him another one from the bag, which disappeared down his throat in a hurry.

Then the rest of Claude's flock flew down from the trees and were at my feet, eyeing the bag of circus peanuts. "Okay, okay," I said, dumping out the peanuts onto the ground beside me. "There's enough for everybody." The birds attacked the peanuts in a heap of beaks and feathers and then snatched the empty bag from my hand. "Hey!"

They fought over the bag for a while until it was

CHAPTER
16

"WAIT HERE, CLAUDE," I SAID, TRYING OUT HIS NEW NAME. "I HAVE something else for you." I crawled into my rock shelter and grabbed the things I'd taken from the campsite. Back outside, I dropped the backpack and diary onto the ground and opened the bag of circus peanuts.

Right away, Claude flew to the backpack. He stuck his head in it.

"Hey! Get out of there!" I stomped my feet. The bird responded by worming his body the rest of the way in. "There's nothing in there for you, Claude! But look here." I shook the circus-peanuts bag. "Here's something you can have."

nothing but a pile of shredded plastic. "You're as hungry as I am." I bent over to pick up the shreds, and when I stood upright again, there was such a pain in my head. I stuffed the plastic into the backpack and said, "I'm as thirsty as a desert, so unless you brought me something to drink, I need to go back to Horace's for some water."

I started to zip up the backpack when I remembered the diary. I picked it up by its cover, and when I did, a piece of paper fell out. It landed at my feet. I unfolded the paper. On it was a charcoal drawing of a big house with a wide porch and tall shutters. A cornfield was sketched on one side and on the other, a creek or stream; it was hard to tell which.

The drawing was fine as drawings go, but you could tell it wasn't done by an artist with much schooling. No doubt Mr. Claude Monet would have said it was worthy of a knifing and a bonfire.

There was something familiar about the house on the map, though. At first I didn't know what, but then I realized. The wide porch. Tall shutters. It was the house I had seen in the memories. The farmhouse where Horace and Magda lived. "This is the map that Horace and Charlie were talking about. It is, isn't it?"

Claude screeched at me. *Rrack-rrack-rrack.*

From the back of the house, there was a dotted line that went across the creek and curved off the paper and onto the other side. I turned the paper over and traced the line with my finger until it ended beside a scribbly blob marked *weeping willow*. Right underneath the weeping willow was a drawing of a box. It had something marked on the top. The something on top looked like the letter "C."

Deep inside my pocket, where the fortune was tucked away, I could feel the heartbeat thumping against my leg. "Uncover your destiny," I said out loud. I looked at Claude. "And this has to be the box that Magda found at Charlie's house, right? She must've taken it. This is what Charlie and Horace have been looking for?"

Claude flew onto my arm. I held still. He was very heavy. He looked at me with his one eye.

"I don't know why I keep asking you questions, because you won't answer. But it doesn't matter. This has got to be what you want me to find. What's buried there by the weeping willow. That's my destiny. And that's what will break the curse."

I didn't just think it; I *believed* it.

I looked at the map again for a clue about where the house might be. There weren't any houses on the mountain that I'd ever come across. But the creek on the map had to be Whistling Creek. It was the only water on all of Smite Mountain. "Okay, change of plans. I'm going back to the creek. And I think I'll be able to find the house from there."

Claude flew off my arm and into the sky.

I folded the map and slid it into my pocket. Then I adjusted the backpack on my shoulders and tramped east through the woods.

I walked fast. I touched the trunks of the trees as I passed them. The trees were old, and they grew close together. Their roots stretched out like long, gnarled fingers on the forest floor and then disappeared deep underground. I wondered how far they had to go to find what they were looking for.

I wondered how far I would have to go.

I tried not to think about what would happen if I couldn't break the curse.

My mama couldn't do it. She tried, but she couldn't. Why did the birds think I could?

Don't lose heart. I could almost hear Toot's gravelly voice. She would be so surprised when she found out what's been going on here while she's been away. *If* she came back. *What if she was so hurt by what I said to her that she decides I'm not worth coming back for?*

"Don't lose heart." I said it out loud as I pulled the fortune from my pocket and felt for its pulse. I wanted to *keep* heart, but how? I closed my eyes and pressed my fingers deeper into the words on the paper until I could feel its heart beating. Was it my imagination, or was the heartbeat slower? And weaker?

I'd never been so good at keeping heart. At the end of the school year in Mr. Desmond's science class, I even lost Resusci Anne's heart when I was learning how to do CPR. I had pressed my hands everywhere on that dummy's rubbery neck, trying to feel the heartbeat under my fingers, but no matter how hard I pushed, nothing came through. "The idea is to save Anne," Mr. Desmond had told me, "not crush her trachea." Everybody laughed except me and Anne. "Uninterrupted chest compressions of one hundred to one hundred twenty a minute until paramedics arrive. Keep that heart going. If you don't, the brain doesn't get enough oxygen, and our dearest, darling Anne will succumb to death in eight minutes. And we don't want that, do we?"

I shook my head. *Succumb* was such a deathly word. It made me think of bony fingers pulling me into the dirt.

I had readied my hands into position over the dummy's chest as Mr. Desmond set the needle on the spinning record. "This Beatles song is in the same tempo as the chest compressions," he shouted over the music. "All you have to do, Cutie Grackle, is keep the beat."

I locked my arms.

The music was loud. Mr. Desmond sang along and marched around the desks in the classroom.

I got to work on Anne's heart. Down. Up. Down. Up. Down. Up.

The song was, as best as I can remember, about two people who were on their way home. The rest of the class clapped along to the music and whooped and hollered. They got behind Mr. Desmond and marched too, like it was some sort of parade. I might have clapped, whooped, and hollered too, if I hadn't been desperately trying to keep Anne from succumbing.

When the song was over, I tried to find Anne's heartbeat. I pressed my fingers so deep, deep, deep into the dummy's thick neck, but there was nothing. I couldn't save her.

Now, to the rhythm of the heartbeat in the fortune inside of my pocket, I marched through the woods toward the creek. I had my own parade, and I swore I'd keep the heartbeat going. I swore that this time I wouldn't lose it.

I would break that curse.

CHAPTER 17

I HAD JUST PASSED AN OLD SYCAMORE WHEN THE BIRDS STARTED making a terrible ruckus.

Then I heard a voice.

"You decided to come out from hiding, huh?" The boy from the camper was sitting on the other side of the sycamore's enormous trunk with Mr. Pitts wedged between his sneakers.

I froze. "What?" I said, even though I'd heard him just fine.

"You decided to come out from hiding. I saw you last night at my campsite stealing our stuff, and I came to find you and get it back."

I wanted to make myself small. *A baby mouse, a*

walnut, a kernel of corn, a grain of wheat, a piece of dirt, a
speck of dust. A baby mouse, a walnut . . .

I wanted to be small enough to stick to the bottom of his shoe, where he couldn't see me. But since that didn't happen, I kept my eyes on the tree roots under my feet.

The boy stood up and leaned against the trunk of the tree. "I found that, uh, hut up there on the cliff. It's the only place I came across on the mountain, and I figured you must live there. I knocked on the door, but you wouldn't answer. I thought taking the elf might bring you out. And here you are."

"Gnome," I corrected, stealing a glance at him. I didn't like it when people got the wrong idea about me, and I supposed Mr. Pitts wouldn't care for it too much either. But whether this boy heard me or not, I didn't know because he kept right on jib-jabbering away.

"So you live up there? No offense, but that place looks like . . . I mean, how do you . . . Uh, do you live there by yourself? What, just you and the elf?"

I said it louder this time. "Gnome."

"What?" he asked.

"He's a gnome, not an elf. There's a big difference."

"Oh." He picked up Mr. Pitts, flipped him upside down, and shook him like he was trying to get a pebble out of an old boot. "If you say so."

"Don't," I said, looking at the boy's face. "He's really old and has a bunch of cracks already. Give him back."

He turned Mr. Pitts right-side up again, then looked at him real close, like he was thinking hard about whether he was going to return him to me.

"He belongs to me," I said.

"Look, I have no interest in keeping your *gnome*. This thing's really heavy. I got tired of carrying it." He shifted Mr. Pitts toward me, and I pulled him close, inspecting him for new cracks.

"I'll take my backpack now," he said.

I took the bag off my shoulder and held it out for him.

It took him a few steps, and they were lopsided. He grabbed the backpack by the metal anchor on the zipper pull and then drew it close to him. I didn't mean to stare at his limping leg, but I couldn't help it. Or maybe I could, I wasn't sure.

He unzipped the backpack and checked inside. He pulled out the handful of shredded plastic that used to be the circus-peanuts bag. He looked at me like I had done it. "Where's the food?"

I didn't say anything because for one thing, I didn't think he'd like the answer I was going to give, and for another thing, all I could think about was that one of his legs was a lot shorter than the other.

He caught me staring, and he stiffened his back. "What?"

"Nothing," I said, quickly looking away.

"You're staring," he said.

"No, I'm not," I said, and right then I was really trying not to.

People aren't paintings to be looked over, Toot had said. *With people, it's what you don't see that tells you more about them than what you do.*

I forced my eyes to look somewhere else and stay there. They settled on Mr. Pitts. "Your diary's in there." I stole a glance at the boy.

"My *what*?" He made a face. "It's not a diary. It's a *chronicle*. There's a big difference."

I shrugged. "If you say so."

"Hey, wait," he said, pointing his finger at me. "You didn't read any of it, did you?"

My cheeks burned.

"You did!" He squeezed his eyes shut and worked his face into a grimace. "Oh man, you read it, I know you did. That totally stinks."

I felt like dirt. I wished I *was* dirt so that I could sink into the ground and not have to talk to him anymore.

"Do you always go around stealing other people's stuff?" he asked.

I felt a twinge of anger rise up in my throat. "No." I hiked up Mr. Pitts in my arm. "Do you?"

"No," he said.

I didn't know where to put my eyes. They drifted back to his legs.

"You're staring again," he said.

I fixed my eyes on Mr. Pitts's pointy hat. There.

"I know you want to know, so ask me," he said.

I kept quiet. Not that I didn't have a lot of questions. I wanted to ask him about the map. I wanted to find out where he got it, and if he knew where the house was. I also wanted to know what happened to his legs. And about the things he wrote in his diary.

But I wasn't used to talking to people who weren't ceramic or Toot.

"Everybody stares," he said. "Everybody wants to know. But go ahead, don't you want to be the first person in human history to just ask?"

When he put it that way, it did sound like a good idea. Who wouldn't want to be the first person in human history to do something? But instead of asking him all the things I wanted to know, including about the house on the map, I asked him the first question that came into my head: "If a tree falls in the forest, and nobody is around to hear it, does it make a sound?"

CHAPTER 18

"OF COURSE NOT," THE BOY SAID RIGHT AWAY. WITHOUT EVEN having to think about it. Like he'd been asked that question a bazillion times before. "Sound waves travel into the ear as vibrations and go all the way through the ear canal, and then the part of the brain that's in charge of hearing recognizes it as sound. So if nobody's around when the tree falls, then there are no ears. And if there are no ears, there's no sound."

No ears, no sound. Well, if that wasn't a turd sandwich.

"Did you know that the stapes is the smallest bone in the human body?" he said. "It's three times the length of a grain of sand."

"I don't think that's right," I told him, still thinking about the tree. "It can't be."

"Well, it is," he said. "You can look it up. The stapes is in the ear, and even though it's really small, if it's damaged from a head injury or something, you can lose your hearing."

"No, not that," I said. "I meant about the tree falling." The tree had to make a sound. It had to. The tree wasn't any less of a tree just because it was all alone. The tree mattered.

The boy shifted his legs. I didn't mean to stare. Again.

He saw. "What?"

"Nothing," I said, looking away.

"Look, I was captured by a gang of outlaws last year. They held me ransom for a month. Demanded a fortune from my mom and pop. And kept me in the badger-infested basement of an abandoned warehouse until they paid up." He squinched up his mouth when he talked, as if each word tasted like horseradish. "That was *badger*-infested, in case you didn't hear right. Not *rats*. Badgers! They are much more dangerous. Have you ever come face-to-face with a badger?"

I swallowed. "No. What are their faces like?"

"And then they put me in some kind of medieval torture contraption," he said, ignoring me. "It pulled and twisted and pulled and twisted and pulled my leg until my muscles tore and bones broke, and when they finally let me out of that thing, my leg was about six whole inches longer than the other one." He slapped his right leg.

I stared at his leg again; I really couldn't help it. I didn't believe him. Of course I didn't. Who would? But one leg was definitely longer than the other. I could see that was true with my own eyes. Maybe not six inches longer, but still.

He raised his eyebrows. "Now tell me that's not the saddest story you ever heard in your life?"

I could tell him a few sad stories of my own. Ones that happened for real.

"You don't believe me?" he asked.

I shook my head.

"I swear it's true. It *is*." His eyes were serious, and he stared at me like he was trying to commandeer my brain with his own. Then his shoulders sagged, and he broke his stare. "Oh fine. It could've been true, you know. Just because I'm interested, which part didn't you buy?"

I shifted Mr. Pitts in my arms. "The part about the badgers," I told him, "in a basement."

"But the badgers are my favorite part."

What did you say to a boy who told lies about badgers? I didn't know. "Okay, well, good," I said. "So you've got your backpack and diary. Bye." I started off with Mr. Pitts.

"Wait! How do you know your way around here? There's no trails or anything. These woods must go on for miles."

"They do," I said. "For fifteen miles." Trees, as far as I could see, in every direction.

"It all looks the same to me. I would've left bread-crumbs or something to find my way back," he said with a nervous laugh, "but you stole all my circus pea-nuts. And my compass." He flipped through the pages of his diary and he pressed his lips together in a tight line. Then he held out his hand. "Okay, hand it over."

"I don't have the circus peanuts," I told him. "Or the compass."

He shook his head. "No, the map. I know you have it."

"What map?" My eyes found the ground again.

"Oh come on," he said. "The map! The one that was inside my chronicle. The one you stole!"

I looked at his face. He was sweaty. He had dirt on his forehead in the shape of an apple. "Where'd you get it, anyway?"

"Ah, so you admit you have it." He wiped his face with the shoulder of his T-shirt, and the apple changed to a breadstick. "Not that it's any business of yours, but I found it. My pop is looking for a prehistoric site for his job. He's a professor of archaeology at West Virginia University. Yesterday I went exploring while he was digging a test unit. And there it was." He stuck out his open hand even closer to me.

Archaeology. Test units. I was trying to follow, but I was thirsty and my head hurt. "You mean you're digging for dinosaur bones?"

"No, that's paleontology. My pop's an *archaeologist*. You know, arrowheads, pottery, stone tools, stuff like that. I usually stay home with my mom when my pop goes out on digs," he said, looking at the ground. "But they thought it would be a good idea if I helped him this time."

So that explained the holes. They didn't have anything to do with the curse. The birds must've known this boy had the map, and they wanted me to find it.

"Hello?" He was snapping his fingers at me. "Are you there?"

"Huh?" I wasn't listening to whatever he was talking about.

The boy shifted his legs and winced. "So what I was saying was that my pop's writing a book on the Fort Ancient people."

"Uh-huh, the Fort Ancient people," I repeated, but my thoughts stayed on the map and finding the house so I could find the weeping willow.

"Don't worry, most people don't know about them either," he went on. "It's not like they make it into schools. History is written by the winners, not the ones who had everything taken from them." He shook his head. "Anyway, the Fort Ancient people are what archaeologists call the Indigenous people who lived along the rivers here about a thousand years ago. Not too much is known about them because by the time the Europeans invaded their land, they disappeared."

"Disappeared?" That got my attention.

"Right," he said. "Disappeared. My pop wants to find out about them so that people will know the real history of this place."

"And you found the map buried in one of the holes you dug?" I asked.

"No, I found it in an old root cellar. It was in a jar, buried all the way in the back. Probably belonged to whoever lived in the house."

"The house?" I said, grabbing his arm. "Is it the house on the map?"

"Um, the house is pretty much gone. All that's left is the foundation. It probably burned down a long time ago."

The knots inside me got tighter. "Burned down? Are you sure?"

He shrugged. "I mean, I think so. That's what it looked like to me. But anyway, I'm pretty sure it's the house on the map. I tried to follow it to the treasure, but I couldn't find the weeping willow. I was going to go back today to try again, but I didn't have my map. Because *someone* broke into our campsite last night and took it."

I wondered if it was true about the fire. When did it happen? In the memory from the fortune, the house was still there. I saw it. Horace and my mama were living there then. That was ten years ago. So it must've happened sometime after that.

He looked at me holding on to his arm. And then he said, "Can you let go?"

"Sorry," I said, removing my hand.

If I got to where the house was, I knew I could find where the box with the "C" was buried. I pulled out the map from my pocket and unfolded it.

"My map!" he said. "Okay, you can hand it over any day now."

I pressed the map against my stomach. "Is it close to your campsite? The foundation of the house?"

"Look, it's *my* map," he said. "I found it. So whatever's buried there under that tree belongs to me."

"No, it doesn't."

"What do you mean, 'No, it doesn't'?" he asked.

I couldn't tell him about the birds. Or the curse. Or the heartbeating fortune. For one thing, he wouldn't believe me, and I couldn't blame him. Even if he did, who's to say I could trust him? He lied about his legs. And he stole Mr. Pitts. Those were two very untrustworthy things.

I pointed to the weeping willow on the map. "See, there's a 'C' on the box that's buried, isn't there?"

"Yeah, so?"

"So," I said, "your name's Galen Podarski, right? I mean, that's the name in the diary."

"Chronicle!"

I ignored him. "So it can't belong to you. It belongs to someone else."

"Who?" he said. "You? What's your name?"

I hadn't thought of it before. How my name started with "C," too. Even though I knew the "C" was for Charlie Mullet, Galen didn't. "My name is Cutie Grackle," I told him.

He laughed and then tried to swallow it. Big surprise. Most kids made fun of me when they found out my name. *Cutie-no-beauty. Cootie bug. Circle, circle, dot, dot, now you have the Cutie shot.* I'd heard them all.

Grown-ups had a different reaction. They would screw up their faces and say, "Aw, now that is just so precious." Then they'd look me over, trying to find an ounce of cuteness that could have inspired such a name. They never found any, I could tell. And that was fine by me.

"Cutie? For real?" he asked after he got his laughing mostly under control. "That's your actual name? I mean that's what's on your birth certificate?"

"I guess." I'd never actually seen my birth certificate, if I even had one.

"No offense or anything, it's just that you don't hear the name Cutie a lot. Or, ever."

No kidding. "Can you just tell me where the house was?"

He shook his head. "Not a chance. But how about this? If you can get me to my campsite, I can *show* you. Deal?"

Well, wonders never cease. The girl found the map.

At last.

In all my days, I never thought I'd have to concern myself over maps and curses and children. I'd rather be picking through a Dumpster or playing stick-catch or making trouble for crows. And yet, here I am.

But I am old. I am nearing the end. And there is a curse to deal with.

I have no use for curses. Curses dwell too much in the what was.

I prefer to consider the what is.

The what is *right now is this: The girl and boy are arguing over the map.*

And this: Horace and Charlie. I hear them.

Their voices skim the wind. Faintly, I can hear their clumsy steps on the forest floor.

The trees whisper to one another. They are coming. They are coming.

They're getting closer to her.

Closer to the girl.

Quickly, I pass the last item from my collection—a broken piece of ceramic—to one of my flock, the raven with blue eyes.

She watches me closely. She can see that I am fading.

I tell her to take the ceramic piece to the girl.

Now.

It's the last memory I have to impart. The last chance to make her understand.

The raven's wings quiver. She knows what I have to do.

I will deal with them.

I will deal with Horace and Charlie.

going to happen tonight, and there was no time to lose.

So I agreed.

We started off. Sometimes I got too far ahead and had to wait for him to catch up. Every so often I asked him if he wanted to stop and take a rest, and he said no like he was bothered by me asking. So I quit asking. And I quit waiting for him too.

He talked nonstop. I mean, this boy could fill up the sky with all of his words. So I kept on walking at my usual pace, and when it got hard for me to hear him, I knew I had gotten too far ahead, and I slowed my steps. That's how we went through the woods together, me and him.

Sometimes I listened to him talking but mostly I was wondering about the house where Horace and Magda grew up and what had happened to it. And what had happened to my mama and the rest of my family. *Did the curse start way back when the Fort Ancient people lived? What started it?* That got me thinking about what this boy wrote in his diary.

"Is it true about the butterfly causing a hurricane on the other side of the world?" I asked him.

CHAPTER 19

WASN'T SO SURE ABOUT LETTING GALEN SHOW ME WHERE THE house on the map was. I didn't know him. And when you don't know someone, you don't know someone.

Plus, he made up stuff. All the things he said about his legs weren't true. Badgers? Really? Toot would say that he talks with his tongue out of his shoe. So how was I supposed to believe that he really had found the house? Or anything else that he said?

But he did have the map. So I figured that if he was telling the truth about where he found it, and it was a very big *if*, I'd get there a lot quicker than if it was just me trying to find the place on my own. Whatever was going to happen with the curse, it was

"You mean the butterfly effect?" he said. "That's what some people believe."

"How does it work?"

"Basically, it means that one small thing, like a butterfly flapping its wings, can cause another thing to happen, and then another, and on and on, until a big thing happens like a hurricane on the other side of the world. So everything can be traced back to a series of events, starting with the butterfly."

"Do you believe it?" I asked, looking back at him.

He shrugged. "I tell you what: I believe the reason I got lost is because all these trees look the same. And the reason I'm out here in the first place is because you stole this." He pointed to his backpack.

My face went hot. I had only taken the backpack to carry the food. And I had only taken his food because the birds stole my chokecherries. And I only picked the chokecherries because Horace let Charlie take everything I got from the pantry. And Charlie was around because he and Horace were looking for what was buried by the willow tree.

If all this happened for a reason, then the reason went back to the curse. Only, it wasn't small like the butterfly.

The curse was the hurricane.

I was starting to feel hungry again. I chewed on my gum extra hard and tried to imagine that I was eating some of that cake I had gotten from the pantry. The blue icing, so sweet it hurt my teeth.

The longer we walked, the heavier Mr. Pitts got. I shifted him from arm to arm, but the rough edge of his coat kept rubbing against my skin, and I finally couldn't take it anymore. We were getting close to a rock formation I knew about, which I called G.H.B. because it was a huge rock that looked like the back end of a horse. G.H.B. Giant Horse Butt. The trouble was, that G.H.B. was a good ways north of the creek, and we were headed east.

I stopped and waited for Galen to catch up. "Look," I said to him. "I can't carry my gnome all the way to your campsite. He's too heavy. There's a place up ahead where I can leave him so that I can find him again."

"Why can't you just leave him here?" said Galen, panting hard.

"Because there's nothing but trees and no marker here, and it'll take me forever to find him again."

He arched his back and winced. "All right," he said. "Let's go."

He didn't understand. "No, I mean, you can just wait here. I'll drop him there and come right back for you."

Galen shook his head. "Are you kidding? You're not leaving me here."

"Why not?" I asked. "There's no point in us both walking there and then having to backtrack to the creek, when I can just go faster on my own."

He winced like I had punched him in the gut.

I didn't realize what I'd said until I said it.

"Right, I'll just slow you down." He looked at his legs and then shifted the weight of his backpack on his shoulders.

"I didn't mean—"

He didn't let me finish. "How do I know you'll come back for me? How do I know you won't just leave me here forever?"

"Because I said I'd come back," I told him. "I don't lie."

That must've zapped him pretty good because he looked both surprised and offended. "Fine," he said, "but I'll hold on to the map." He held out his hand. "And just so you know, I don't lie. I make things up. There's a big difference."

There was no time for arguing. I dug the map from my pocket and handed it to him. "Stay right here."

He said, "Where do you expect me to go?"

I walked as fast as a person carrying a ceramic garden gnome with an attitude could. Mr. Pitts weighed a ton. And he complained the whole way.

"I can't believe you let that boy steal me," he said. "And did you see the way he turned me upside down? Madness! I might as well be back in the shed."

"I'm sorry," I told him.

"You're sorry? My dear girl, until you've been sto- len, stuffed under an armpit for a long journey into the woods, mistaken for an elf, and then flipped upside down like a piggy bank, you don't know sorry from a sailboat."

I was pretty sure I did know sorry from a sailboat. I knew lots of things. I knew that Mr. Pitts should at least appreciate the fact that I said I was sorry, when none of the things that happened to him were really my fault, anyhow. Nobody ever said sorry for all the things that happened to me. But if they did, and if they meant it, I think it would make me feel a little better, at least.

We finally got to G.H.B. I had just tucked Mr. Pitts between two sturdy boulders at the base when a raven swooped down and landed on one of the boulders. This raven was smaller than Claude, and when I got closer, I noticed its eyes were blue. "Where's Claude?" I asked.

As usual, the bird said nothing.

Then it rapped its beak against the rock and opened it wide. A small, hard thing fell out of it. The thing was brown. One side was flat, and the other was long and curved.

I stepped closer. I could hardly believe what I was looking at, because what I was looking at was a nose. A ceramic one. Right away I knew it belonged to Mr. Pitts.

"Murderation!" I said. "How did you . . . I mean, do you know . . . this is . . . Where did you get this?"

I stared at the nose. It was such a tiny thing.

"Is this going to show me something like the other things did? A memory?"

The bird just watched me with its blue eyes.

"Right," I said to myself. "Stop asking them questions."

I picked up the nose and squeezed it tight in my hand.

Right away, everything blurred at the edges and faded away. Then, as things slowly became clear again, I saw a small stone cottage at the top of a mountain. It was night. I stood in front of the cottage, and the full moon shined on the front yard, which was packed with flowering trees, huckleberry bushes, and lawn orna-mentals—fairies, jigglers, nest boxes, gazing globes, whirligigs, and one winking gnome.

Mr. Pitts!

He stood directly under a window. His painted coat was bright green, and he looked to have fewer cracks running through him. Most importantly, his nose was on his face, in the exact place where you'd expect to see it.

I started toward him when a raven flew out of a huckleberry bush. It landed next to a pair of pruning shears that had been left on the windowsill above Mr. Pitts. I recognized the bird when I saw his one eye. It was Claude.

Just then, the door to the cottage flew open and out stepped an old lady. She wore light-colored overalls rolled up so high, I could see her thick knees. Her gray hair was piled in a messy heap on top of her head. Two feathers were sticking out of the heap in opposite directions. It was hard to tell if they were put there on purpose or if she had just wrestled a peacock.

By the looks of her, both things seemed possible.

She was holding a telephone up to her ear and twirling the long cord that trailed like a fishing line into the cottage. "Mr. Miller," the lady said into the telephone, "this is Pearlie Mae Grouse. Yes, I am aware that it's almost midnight. And yes, I am aware that it's the second time I've called you this week at this hour."

Pearlie Mae? I thought. *I've heard that name before.*

A small dog with a smushed-in face trotted out the door of the cottage and sniffed at the grass near the lady's feet.

"Mr. Miller," said the woman called Pearlie Mae, "the strangest thing happened. I awoke with a severe hankering for crabapple jam." She nodded at the voice on the telephone and paced in the grass. "You are absolutely correct. A severe hankering cannot and should not be ignored. The problem is, Mr. Miller, that my sugar bowl is empty. Indeed it is! And you cannot make crabapple jam without sugar. It would be a travesty." She switched the telephone to her other ear. "Yes, well, I thought you might. How lucky I am, Mr. Miller, that you live just at the bottom of the hill. Monte and I will be down shortly. Goodbye."

She went back inside the house to hang up the telephone. When she returned, she was holding a sugar canister under her arm. She called to her dog, Monte, who was at her ankles immediately. They walked through the front yard, side by side, and onto a gravel road. I followed close behind, and I noticed Claude flying low, just ahead of us.

Pearlie Mae looked up at the full moon. "They call that a Rose Moon," she told Monte. "Personally, I prefer forsythias to roses."

They walked on down the hill and passed a metal gate. A good ways behind the gate was a wooden barn and four huge storage tanks. On each tank was painted:

160

Bootstrap Molasses Company

Gypsum, West Virginia

"Out late tonight, aren't you, Pearlie Mae?" said a man leaning on the gate. He was wearing dark blue coveralls and smoking a cigar.

"Indeed I am, Mr. Blumby," she replied. "There's no time to waste when you're trying to prevent a travesty from occurring."

"A travesty, huh?" he said, laughing. "What sort of travesty happens at midnight?"

"Oh, one you wouldn't understand, Mr. Blumby."

"Crazy old bird," he muttered.

Pearlie Mae walked right on by without paying him any mind, but Monte lifted his leg on the gate's lower rail.

Moments later, a whistle sounded from somewhere on the Bootstrap Molasses Company property. And then an explosion. I covered my ears it was so loud. Pearlie Mae stumbled. Monte whined and cowered behind her.

I saw it happen. The storage tanks, one after another, splitting apart. Then a wave of molasses the size of a house barreling down the hill. "Watch out!"

I yelled at Pearlie Mae. But she didn't hear me. She couldn't, because I wasn't really there. There was no time for watching out, anyway. Pearlie Mae picked up Monte just as the giant wave swallowed the factory and everything in its path, including Mr. Blumby, Monte, Pearlie Mae Grouse, and her severe hankering for crabapple jam.

They were gone. Just like that. At midnight.

Midnight! *Is that when the curse happened?*

Then the molasses river that swept through the mountain faded away in front of my eyes, and I was back at the top of the mountain in the front yard of Pearlie Mae's cottage. The explosion had caused most of the ornamentals in her yard to topple over. Whirligigs, fairies, and jigglers were broken. Nest boxes were un-nested. Claude had returned too and was standing on top of a gazing globe that had been knocked off its stand. He was joined by another raven, who was perched on top of Mr. Pitts's pointy hat.

Poor Mr. Pitts. The pruning shears that had been on the windowsill above him were now at his feet, along with his broken-off nose. I saw Claude fly over to the nose and snatch it up with his beak. Then he and the other raven disappeared into the night.

I was glad when that memory was over and I was back at the G.H.B. I'd never been so happy to see the Giant Horse Butt. The raven with blue eyes was still here. It hopped onto the toe of my shoe and started pecking at the metal eyelet around my shoelaces. I let it. What did I care?

It was a terrible thing to see somebody get swallowed up by molasses. A terrible, terrible thing. It was bad enough to hear a stranger at the food pantry tell you about mysterious deaths and disappearances on the mountain, but to see it happen with your own eyes!

I felt heavy, like someone had dumped a pile of curtains on top of me. The thick, dusty kind that blocked out the sun. It was hard to breathe under curtains.

"That poor Pearlie Mae woman," I said, when I could catch my breath. "And her little dog. All that molasses." And then I realized. "Murderation! So that's why the mountain sometimes smells like pancakes!"

I also remembered where I had heard that name. In the memory from the fortune, my mama said that she had lost so much. *First Grandma Pearlie Mae, she had said.* Pearlie Mae must've been my mama's grandmother. Which meant that she was my great-grandmother! Mama also said that she had lost "Mother and Pa." My grandparents. *Did the curse take them too?*

Something inside me told me *yes*.

I knew I wouldn't get an answer from the raven, but I couldn't help myself. "But why is there a curse in the first place?"

The raven, who was busy stripping my shoelace from my shoe, stopped for a moment and looked up at me with its blue eyes.

"Something must've caused the curse, right?" I didn't know much about the inner workings of curses, but I knew they didn't just show up on their own and for no reason.

There was only a tiny end of my shoelace threaded through the last eyelet on my shoe. Instead of giving me an answer, the bird pulled my shoelace free with its beak and took it away into the trees.

made it back, he said, "What took you so long? Did you hear that? I heard . . . I mean, it sounded like . . . and, Cutie, I swear I'm not lying—"

"I heard it too," I told him. Then I sat on the ground to catch my breath.

He was hugging his backpack to his chest. "Where'd it come from?"

"I don't know," I said. "Somewhere down the mountain."

"Like where we're headed?"

"I don't think so," I said, even though it was impossible to know. "It was probably just someone out hunting."

"Okay, right," he said. "Hunting." He loosened his grip on the backpack. "That makes sense. Hunting. Okay."

"Look," I said, "we need to get going. What time is it?"

He shrugged. "My watch is back at the camper. But I'm pretty sure I left our campsite at one thirty, after my pop went into town. And it took me a while before I found you. So I don't know. But it's got to be close to dinnertime, because I'm starving."

For once, I wasn't thinking about my stomach. I was thinking about finding that weeping willow before midnight. "Come on, we've got to go." I held out my hand.

He looked at me and made a face like he thought I wanted him to take my hand. "Um . . ."

My cheeks burned. I pulled my hand away and hid it behind my back. "No, no, no. That's not what I meant. I mean, I'll take the map back now. Give it to me. In my hand."

"Oh right. The map." He cleared his throat. "You don't trust me, do you?"

I decided not to say anything.

"What? It's not like I'm going to run off or anything," he said, pointing to his legs. "Tell you what, you get me back to my campsite, and I'll let you hold on to the map. Deal?"

I eyeballed him up and down. "And you'll show me where you found the map? Where the foundation of the house is, right?"

"Promise," he said, smiling.

Charlie Mullet might've been some good shot when he was young, but over the years his aim has gotten quite poor. The bullet whizzes past me, and I abruptly change direction. I climb higher, forcing the air down with my wings.

The air feels heavier. Or is it me?

I'm slipping. It takes every bit of strength to climb.

Horace and Charlie are below me. They smell sour, like an egg that will never hatch but has stayed too long in the nest.

"What'd you do that for, Charlie?" asks Horace.

"Shut up, Horace. I got a feeling the birds are working with the girl. Just like they were doing with your sister. I ain't gonna let them find it before we do."

When I can climb no more, I tuck in my wings and let gravity draw me down. I pick up speed. Keeping my wings close to my body, I use my tail to maneuver turns. The trees know my intentions, and they let me through.

I barrel toward Horace and Charlie.

The wind is thick. It pushes against me. Cuts my speed.

I extend my wings at the last possible moment and break my dive. I level off and thrust forward, darting between Horace and Charlie.

"Get it!" yells Charlie.

I tear past them.

And they follow. I can hear them behind me, fumbling over tree roots.

Just a bit farther. *I tell my heart to steady on.* Just a bit farther. Just a bit.

CHAPTER 21

WE STARTED OFF AGAIN, DOWN THE MOUNTAIN TOWARD WHISTLING Creek. I was so thirsty, even if I drank all the water in the creek I wasn't sure it'd be enough. I kept a lookout for any sign of Claude and his flock, or for Horace and Charlie. I didn't tell Galen, but I had a very bad feeling that Charlie had shot off that gun. And wherever Charlie was, Horace was right there with him.

They were out looking for the same thing we were—whatever it was that my mama had taken from Charlie's house ten years ago and buried by the weeping willow.

But what I didn't understand was this: Why did Charlie have the thing that would undo the curse in the first place?

I tried to make my pace slow so Galen could keep up, but if I was going to find the weeping willow and dig up my destiny before midnight, there was no time for slowness.

"There's no trails. No signs," said Galen after a while. "Nothing but trees that all look the same. I mean, it's no wonder I got turned around."

"Hemlock," I said as we passed one.

"What?" he said.

"American pine. Cypress."

"Um, what are you doing?" asked Galen.

"Naming the trees," I answered. "You said they all looked the same. They don't, really."

"Sure, they don't," he said. "Tall, brown trunks; green leaves; homes to squirrels. You're right, they are so different."

I didn't say anything.

"Hey," said Galen, hurrying his steps and closing the distance between us. "I didn't mean to laugh at your name before. I've just never met anybody named Cutie." He stumbled over a fallen branch but regained his footing. "Not that Galen is a super common name either. There's only one other kid named Galen at my school, and she's a girl. But that's okay, because there's also Galen Erso."

He waited for me to say something. I didn't.

"You know, Galen Erso? The scientist from *Star Wars*. Galen. Erso. You know, the guy that sabotaged the Death Star by putting a weakness in the thermal exhaust port. He's the reason the rebels were able to blow it up!"

I shrugged. "Another American pine. There's another cypress."

"What, you don't like *Star Wars* or something?" he said.

"I don't know," I said. "I've never seen it." I pointed to a tree on the right. "That's a hemlock."

"Wait a second." He took a few quick steps to catch up again. "You've never seen *Star Wars*?"

"Nope."

"I don't mean just the original ones, I mean any of them," he said.

"Nope," I said and then pointed straight ahead. "We're almost to the creek." I walked faster.

"*Star Wars*. The movie."

I stopped and turned to face him. "No, I haven't seen it. Haven't seen *them*. Any of them. None."

"For real?" he said. "I mean, no offense or anything, but how is that possible? *Star Wars* is like . . . it's like . . . a rainbow. A beautiful, galactic, planet-exploding, Millennium Falcon–chasing rainbow. Everybody has seen at least one in their lifetime."

"Not everybody." I started off again and ducked under a heavy curtain of vines.

"Apparently." Galen slowed, putting more space between us. "Wow, never seen *Star Wars*. It's going to take me awhile to process that. Wow."

"You said that already."

"Right, okay, so you haven't seen *Star Wars*. Moving on." He ducked under the vines just as I had done and then hurried to catch up.

Galen talked the whole way to Whistling Creek, about the biting flies and mosquitoes that kept buzzing around his ears, about *Star Wars*, about his move from Baltimore to "this backwoods place," about how one day he was going to do something really important, and how the map was his way to get there.

He sure liked to talk, and I got the feeling he wasn't bothered if I said anything or not, so I didn't.

When we finally made it to Whistling Creek, I plunged into the water, lay down on my stomach, and drank in mouthfuls of the cold creek. After I'd gotten enough and the pain in my head finally went away, I flipped over. Galen was on the bank watching me. "Go ahead," I told him. "I do it all the time. It's safe."

Galen got to his knees. Then he cupped his hands, dipped them into the creek, and gulped.

I watched the sky, keeping lookout for the ravens. But the sky was empty, and the mountain was quiet. I reached my hands into the bottom of the creek bed and felt for smooth pebbles.

"You don't like to talk much, do you?" he asked.

"Not as much as you, I guess."

Galen rubbed his back and winced. "I know I talk a lot. I'd rather people pay attention to the things I say instead of . . ." His voice trailed off. He unfolded his legs from underneath him and let them hang over the side of the creek bed. His one sneaker looked different from the other. I hadn't noticed it before. Like it had two soles glued together. Then I saw that it was the shoe for his short leg, to try to make up some of the difference. But even with the extra soles, his short leg couldn't catch up.

He must've seen me looking because he blurted out, "It's called fibular hemimelia."

"Huh?"

"It means that one of my legs didn't form completely. I had one operation when I was a baby to fix my ankle, and another one when I was four to make the bone in my leg longer." The words raced out of him one right after the other, without a breath in between. When they were all out, he took another scoop from the creek.

"They can make the bone in your leg longer?" I said.

He nodded. "It takes a couple of operations, but yeah. I'm supposed to have another one in a couple of weeks so it will catch up to my normal leg. And then I'll need another one later on."

I'd never heard of such a thing before, and I had my doubts. After all, this was the same boy who told me he was tortured by outlaws and basement badgers. All that wasn't true, so probably this was just another one of his stories.

I stomped through the creek and climbed onto the bank beside him. "We should go."

Galen took one last drink. He had some trouble getting up from his knees, but this time I made a point of not staring and not asking if he needed help.

"How much longer until we're back at my campsite?" he asked, looking in the wrong direction from where we were headed.

"It's that way," I said, pointing down the mountain, "and it's not that far from here." My stomach grumbled. But I ignored it the best I could and instead thought about finding the foundation of the house.

"If my pop gets back and I'm not there," Galen said, "man, I'm going to be in so much trouble." He started off, walking faster than I'd seen him. I matched his pace.

"How come?" I asked.

Galen wiped the sweat from his forehead. "Because my pop was going into town this afternoon for a meeting, and I was supposed to be screening dirt while he was gone. He said he'd be back after four thirty. If he's back and I'm not there, oh man."

"Oh man, what? He'll be mad?"

"Worse than mad," Galen said. "What time do you have to be home?"

"Home?" I asked. "I don't."

"You mean your parents don't care if you're gone all day?" he said. "Lucky."

I didn't say anything. I let him take the lead. The distance between us got bigger.

tree belongs to you because there's a 'C' on the box on the map," said Galen, "but what if the 'C' is for something else. Like, what if it's a box of Confederate coins or something? The map doesn't look that old, though, not Civil War old, so maybe not Confederate money, but maybe the 'C' is for the person who buried it. Or it could be an old war chest full of gold from a colonel in the Civil War."

"What do you mean?"

"Because *colonel* starts with 'C,'" he said. "Also *Civil War*." He frowned like maybe that wasn't such a good example. "Anyway, lots of people's names begin with 'C.' That's my point." He was quiet for a moment and then said, "It . . . it could be . . . um . . . Christopher Columbus. Yeah, or even, um . . . Davy Crockett. Or you know what would be really great? If there was something like the terra-cotta army buried there."

"What's that?"

"The terra-cotta army? Some farmers in China found all these sculptures of soldiers and horses and chariots in the ground near where the first emperor was buried to protect him in the afterlife. They were there for a thousand years or something before anybody found them." His steps got faster. "But you know, if it's anything like that, we can't keep it." He held on to my shoulder as he stepped over a fallen tree. "The place where I found the map, there were a bunch of holes dug already. Looters, probably. People looking for artifacts to sell." Galen shook his head. "But they have no right to take things that don't belong to them. Anything they find there belongs with the Indigenous people."

"What about the map?" I said. "You took that."

"That's different. The map doesn't have any historical importance that we know about. Can we stop for a minute?" He rubbed his back and started to lean against the trunk of a honey locust.

"Watch out," I said, grabbing his arm. He was about a half inch away from backing into a cluster of spiky thorns on the tree.

Galen turned around, and when he spied the thorns he hollered and stumbled backward. "What kind of seriously demented tree is that?"

"Honey locust," I told him. "The thorns are so hard and so sharp that in the olden days, they used them as nails." That's what Toot told me, anyhow.

"That would've seriously hurt," he said. "I mean, that's like the stuff of nightmares."

I nodded. "Best to look before you lean."

"Right," said Galen. "Look, then lean. Got it. So what was I talking about, you know, before this tree almost speared me like a kabob?"

"About how you taking the map isn't the same thing as people who take other stuff they find because it's not important—"

"Oh yeah," he said, "because it's not important in a *historic* way, that's what I meant. I like to find that kind of stuff—you know, the map, glass soda bottles, coat buttons, broken pieces of dinner plates—because even though they don't look like much, a long time ago they meant something to somebody." He reached into his pocket and pulled out a small gold jingle bell. He held it in his palm so I could see. "Like this. I found it in one of the test units we dug. It's not super old or valuable or anything like that, but it belonged to somebody who lived around here. It meant something to them, I bet. And there's a story behind it, do you know what I mean?"

I did know what he meant. Very, very much.

There was something about the bell. It was a tiny little thing and shiny. It was just the kind of thing that a raven might put a memory inside. Galen had the map, and the birds had wanted me to find that. Maybe they wanted me to find this bell too.

Maybe it would show me what started the curse.

I took it from him and squeezed it in my hand.

Nothing happened.

I squeezed harder.

"What are you doing?" asked Galen.

I opened my hand. I looked at the bell and then at Galen. "I thought . . ." I gave the bell back to him. "Never mind."

CHAPTER 23

"**I'M IN TROUBLE.**"

I caught up with him just as he stepped into the clearing. He was staring at his campsite. His father, holding a shovel, was standing next to one of the holes.

"Okay," I said. "I got you here, so I'll take the map now."

But Galen did not give me the map. He did the very thing that was the opposite of map giving. He took off in a sort of run toward the camper.

I ran after him, yelling. "You promised!"

Galen got to the site first. He slowed his steps as he got closer to his father, who was dumping a bucket of dirt onto some kind of screen and pressing it through the mesh holes with his fingers.

I hung back a little and stood next to an old sycamore.

Galen's father looked up when he saw Galen coming. His face was pinched at the sides like he wanted to leap forward but something had hold of his ears. "Where have you been?" he asked, dropping the screen. "It's almost six o'clock."

Six o'clock. Only six more hours until midnight.

"Didn't you get my note?" Galen said to his father.

"Right, the note. I believe it said, 'I'll be back soon.' Do you think that was adequate information? What if you'd gotten lost or if you'd fallen and hurt your legs, Galen? You know you have to be careful. One injury could set back your surgery and throw the entire plan off schedule."

"I know," said Galen. "Sorry."

I peeked around the tree. Galen was staring at the ground. He looked so small next to his father.

"Not to mention the commitment you made to helping me out here. I mean, you do remember the talk we had last night? You were there, right? If it wasn't you, then there's a doppelgänger running around here somewhere on this mountain, and maybe he can help me screen this dirt, which is what you agreed—" Then he must've seen me peeking around the tree, because he said, "I beg your pardon. Who's this?"

Murderation! My eyes darted to Galen's father when he stopped talking. I froze.

"That's Cutie," said Galen. "She lives up here, on the mountain. Cutie, this is my pop."

"Dr. Podarski," he said, pushing his glasses to the top of his nose. He nodded in my direction. "Pleasure."

They both looked at me like they were waiting for me to do something. Or say something. But the thing was, I didn't know what to do or say. So I just pretended to be very fascinated by the bark of the sycamore tree I was standing next to.

Eventually, Galen and his father got back to talking. I listened while I took a close-up examination of the bark. And sometimes stole a glance at them when they weren't looking.

Galen's father cleared his throat. "Son, we had an agreement."

"I know," said Galen. "But what happened was—"

Dr. Podarski held up his hand. "Save the excuses and your grand stories. There's no time. I expect you to catch up on your work this evening. I'm serious. There can be no lollygagging, no more running off, and no excuses. If you're not going to keep your commitments . . ." He squeezed his lips together tight, like he was fighting to keep the rest of the words from shooting out. "What do we say about commitments?"

"Commitment is what transforms a promise into reality," Galen and his pop recited together.

I liked that. Promises should become real. But you had to do something to make them real. Otherwise they were just words. Like when Galen promised to let me have the map if I got him back here. Just words.

"Abraham Lincoln," said Dr. Podarski. "That was a man of strength. Now then, I'll be starting on shovel tests in the southeast corner." He scratched his beard and scanned the trees. "There's significant history here. A story to be told." He picked up a tiny object among the dirt on the screen. He rubbed it on his shirt and then held it in his hand. "What we find here connects us to the past. It may be an ugly,

shameful past, but we have the responsibility of own-
ing up to it so that we can know better and then do
better." He closed his eyes and took in a deep breath.
"I can smell it, can't you? The connection?"

"Definitely," said Galen. "I can smell it." He caught
me looking at them smelling things, and he waved me
closer.

I finished with my pretend examination of the
sycamore bark and went over to Galen and his father.
They wanted me to smell things too, I could tell. I
sniffed the air while they watched me, and I tried to
smell the connection. I really did. But all I could get
was sweat and dirt. And molasses.

Galen gave me a nervous grin. "Cutie wants to
help."

"What?" Dr. Podarski said. He blinked his eyes
like he had just been pulled from a dream. "Yes, well,
fine. She has an interest in learning about the past,
does she?"

I looked at Galen, who was staring at me and nodding. He seemed to be giving mind control another
shot. "Right," I said finally. "I do. Yes. Big interest. In
the past." It wasn't an all-out lie. What happened to

my family, that was in the past. And I was very interested in learning about that.

"We can certainly use some more hands if we are going to stay on schedule. Galen, you can show her what needs to be done."

"Exactly," Galen said to his father, as if that had been the plan all along.

"We've got to stay on course," said Dr. Podarski. "There's no point in having a schedule if you don't stick to it, now is there? We have made a commitment, after all." He picked up a shovel and started off toward a hole. He paused long enough to say, "I bought some sandwiches while I was in town. They're in the camper. Help yourself."

Help yourself. Those two small words hung in the air. I wanted to jump inside them.

Galen headed for the dirt pile. But I didn't follow. "Hey, what's the matter?" he said, looking back.

I felt like a stray dog who'd had a bone waved under its nose and then tossed away. I stared at the silver camper. I might've let out a whimper.

"Oh right," said Galen. "I almost forgot how hungry I was. Do you want something to eat?"

I followed him to the camper, keeping my head down to watch out for holes. But even more to push down the shame that was filling up inside me. I was very hungry and at the same time very ashamed of it. I didn't want Galen, or anybody else, to see.

That was something I wanted to keep buried deep.

CHAPTER 24

GALEN BROUGHT OUT THE GROCERY BAG FROM THE CAMPER AND set it on a small folding table next to two chairs. He unpacked the food and laid it all out on the table. Before I sat down, I watched him choose his sandwich and start to undo the plastic wrapping. He told me to go ahead, and I didn't know what I was waiting for, because I was so hungry and there was a sandwich right in front of me.

It looked like ham and orange cheese.

I loved ham and orange cheese.

"You said you'd hand over the map if I got you here," I reminded him, keeping my eyes on him. Not on the sandwich. "You promised. And I got you here. So give me the map. Please. Now."

I didn't mean for it to come out the way it sounded. Jerky.

"Right," he said, frowning. "That's what I said." He reached into his pocket and handed me the map.

I took it from him and unfolded it to make sure it was just as it was when I left it with him. It was. So I slid it into the front pocket of my pants.

"You don't trust anybody, do you?" he said.

I didn't know what to say to that, but the truth was that people took things. It felt like everything I ever had was taken away.

Galen bit into his sandwich and started talking about *Star Wars*. I had planned to leave as soon as I had the map. But I was hungry. Very, very hungry. And when you're hungry, you do things.

This is what I did: I ate the sandwich.

I ate it in small bites while he talked but was careful not to eat too fast or too much. My stomach wasn't used to getting what it wanted, and if it did, I was afraid it wouldn't know when to stop.

It *was* a ham-and-orange-cheese sandwich. On white bread. With mustard. And there was an extra surprise of a dill-pickle spear tucked inside the wrapping. I loved a surprise pickle. Galen even gave me my very own bag of chips and a bottle of iced green tea. He didn't make a big deal about it either. He just set the chips and tea in front of me without asking.

When half of everything was gone, I made myself stop eating, which wasn't an easy thing to do when my stomach kept talking to my brain and telling it: *More. Don't stop. Don't you know how long it's been?* I rewrapped the half of the sandwich I hadn't eaten in its plastic wrapping, saving it for later. And it was a good thing I did, because I got a really sharp pain in my stomach then. A couple more pains came, and I pressed my hands over my stomach and waited for them to go away. That sometimes happened when I ate after not eating for a while.

When the pain finally passed, I asked Galen if I could borrow the plastic grocery bag. He said I could, and I slipped the leftover food into the bag and calculated in my head how many days I could make it last. Three, maybe four.

But then it occurred to me that when I broke the curse and my family came back, maybe I wouldn't have to worry about making food last anymore.

Galen was watching me, but he didn't say a word.

"So that's your dad," I said, trying to get him talking again so that he wouldn't ask me about my food problem. "He's a doctor too?"

"A doctor? Oh, no, well, yeah, sort of. He's not a *doctor* doctor. He's a *scientist* doctor. Not the kind of doctor you call when you're sick. He's the kind of doctor that you call when you find something old buried in your backyard."

"He seems very responsible," I said.

"Responsible?" He gave me a confused look. "I guess."

"He bought you sandwiches," I said. "And it didn't seem like he was so mad you were gone."

Galen stuck his finger in his mouth and scraped the chunk of sandwich that was lodged in his teeth. "He doesn't get mad. Not really. He gets disappointed, and that's a thousand times worse. He's a big believer in doing what you say you're going to do. He doesn't have time for people who don't honor commitments, because he says they're weak."

"Is that what you believe too?"

"Watch this." He threw a potato chip into the air

and caught it in his mouth. He chewed and swallowed. "I believe in freedom of choice." He threw another chip into the air and caught it between his teeth. "What do you believe in?"

I thought about all the things that I hoped *would be*. "Lots of things," I told him. "Impossible things."

"Like what?" He threw another chip into the air. This time he missed.

I watched the chip land next to his shoe. I wondered if he was going to eat it.

The light was starting to fade, and I was getting anxious. "You said you'd show me where you found the map. Where the foundation of the house is."

Galen's face fell. "I will. But you heard my pop. I need to catch up on the work I was supposed to be doing today."

I couldn't wait that long. I told him that.

"Why can't you wait?" he asked.

"I just can't."

"Come on. Tell me."

I wanted to tell *Toot* about the curse. That's who I wanted to tell. I wanted to tell her about the birds. And the memories. And my destiny. But Toot wasn't here. She was gone, just like everybody else.

I was alone, except for this boy, and I didn't know what to think about him. I didn't trust him, not really. When everybody's left you and you're all alone, the only person you can count on is yourself. So what was the point in telling Galen anything? He wouldn't believe me, and why should I tell him anything about me when all he did was make up things about himself?

The knots inside me were tightening.

"Why can't you wait?" he said again.

I felt a rush of anger in my throat. It stung my eyes. "Because I can't! So can you just tell me where you saw the foundation of the house? I should be able to find the weeping willow from there."

Galen must not have known what to say for once. His mouth was open, and I could see a chunk of sandwich wedged in his teeth.

"Sorry." I stood up and grabbed the bag with my leftover food. "But thank you for the food."

"No way," Galen said, standing up too. "You can't leave. Not without me. I can go, but I need to wait until my pop falls asleep. He always falls asleep during *Jeopardy!* around eight o' clock, so we can go then."

I turned away.

"I know you don't trust me, and I know I make things up, but I gave you the map like I said I would, and that has to count for something. You don't understand. I need to go with you."

It was my turn to ask. "Why?"

He gripped the edge of the table. "Because I'm tired of everybody acting like I don't count. Making decisions for me. Leaving me out. Do you know what that feels like? Being left behind?"

I did know. Everybody I knew was gone. Even Claude had disappeared.

I was afraid I might disappear too.

If a girl disappears in a forest, and nobody is around to notice, does it matter?

"Come on," he said, and he touched my hand. "The foundation of the house isn't that far from here."

The flutter in my chest returned. It was so strong, I thought my heart was going to fly right out of my body.

"Please," he said again. "I'm telling the truth. Can't you see that?"

I thought about what Toot said about being a luminary. Seeing things that nobody else can. But I didn't know if he was telling the truth. And I didn't know if I really had the makings of a luminary. But the flutter in my chest kept on fluttering. Along with it there came a feeling of fullness.

It was a good feeling.

"Okay," I said then. "Okay."

CHAPTER 25

IT WAS ALMOST DARK WHEN WE LEFT THE CAMPSITE, SIDE BY SIDE.
The sky was at least ten shades of blue. Like someone
had painted a stripe of midnight blue at the top and
then watered it down until it faded away into the trees.

Galen and I had packed real fast while the *Jeopardy!*
theme song played from inside the camper. I had the
map and a flashlight that Galen had given me. He put
his trowel and a couple of water bottles into his backpack and took another flashlight from the glovebox in
his pop's truck.

Before we left, I asked him if he had any small
trinkets he could bring along. Something made out
of metal or glass. Things that reflected the light. He

asked me why, and I told him that I would tell him on the way. It would take me a while to explain. He went back inside the camper and brought out a plastic bag of things he had found when he and his pop were digging: a paper clip, a silver button, and a piece of green bottle glass. He slid them into his pocket. I also told him to bring a watch.

And then we left.

The light from our flashlights made two wide circles on the ground in front of us. The circles overlapped on the sides.

Before I told him anything about the curse and the ravens, I needed to know something. "Is it true what you said about the operation to make your leg longer?"

He stopped and rolled up his right pants leg. There were scars on his calf and around his ankle. Some were in the shape of small circles. And there was a short, thin line below his knee. "Yeah, it's true. It's part of the big Podarski plan to fix me."

"Don't you want to have the operation?" I asked.

"You mean, do I want to have legs that are the same size? Yeah. Sure, who wouldn't? But it's not like one surgery and then I'm done, fixed. It's a couple of surgeries, probably three, where my bone is cut and then is pulled apart a little each day so that a new bone can grow in its place. And after every one, it's not being able to walk on my own for about three months. And going back to Baltimore to be near the hospital for a while so that I can have therapy four times a week. And it's wearing an annoying fixator on the outside of my leg with pins that go through my skin and into my bone. For close to nine months. And it's people staring. Even more than they do now." He bent over to undo his rolled-up pants leg. When he straightened up again, he winced like he was in pain, and then he repositioned the way he was standing.

So the part of his badger story about the medieval torture device was true, sort of.

He took in a deep breath and then let it out in a whoosh. "It's not that I don't appreciate what my parents have done for me. You know, to fix my legs. They just never asked me if it's what I wanted. Anyway, it doesn't matter. Everything is already set in motion. There's no changing course now."

I wanted to tell him about this one time that Horace caught a rabbit in the trap. About how the rabbit didn't even try to get free. Didn't even sniff around the edges of the crate to see if there was a way out. It just curled into a ball in the middle of the crate and waited. I had wanted to let the rabbit out so bad so that it could be free, but I didn't do anything but watch from the woodpile. Galen was kind of like that rabbit.

I wanted to tell him that, but I didn't.

Maybe I was like that rabbit too.

Then Galen said, "You really think that whatever is buried by that tree is meant for you?"

I could've gone along with what I told him before, said yes, and just left it at that. I could have. But after he told me the truth about himself, I figured I owed him the truth too. That seemed like the right thing.

It worked that way for the ravens, anyway. The birds gave me something, and I gave them something in return. Or, most of the time they took something from me without my permission. But still. One for one.

So I told Galen everything. I told him about Horace and his dark moods. About Charlie. I told him about the curse and how my whole family had disappeared. Then I told him about Claude and his flock of ravens.

About the fortune they brought me, and the other things too, and about how the objects had memories inside of them somehow. I told him how I was going to break the curse. Because what was buried by the weeping willow tree, in the box that my mama took from Charlie's house, it was my destiny.

I told him all of that while we walked to the place where Galen found the map. The starting point.

Galen was quiet while I was telling him, but he kept looking at me sideways like he wasn't sure he believed me. He was looking at me so much that he wasn't watching where he was going, and he tripped over a rock that was sticking up out of the ground. He caught himself and got back his footing.

Finally, after I was finished with all of the telling, he asked, "And what's buried there?"

"I told you," I said. "My destiny."

"Yeah, but what is it exactly?"

"I don't know. The fortune says 'Uncover your destiny, and you will remake history.'"

Galen made a *pppffffttt* noise and said, "Destiny." He said it the way I say, "Lima beans."

"You don't believe in destiny," I said.

"Well, who wants to live in a world where everything is decided for you already? Where you can't choose to do something, or not to do it, all on your own? Where everything happens for a reason?"

"But what about that butterfly-effect thing?" I asked. "You said yourself that everything happens for a reason."

"No, I said that's what *some* people believe. I'm not some people."

"But why . . ."

"Why was I born with these legs?" he said, interrupting me. "If everything happens for a reason, what's the reason?"

I didn't know.

"There isn't one," he answered for me. "It's just like in *Star Wars* where Darth Vader tells Luke that it's his destiny to join him on the dark side, to rule the galaxy as father and son. But Luke says 'No way' to that. He decides on his own not to turn to the dark side. *And* he saves his father, defeats the emperor, narrowly escapes an exploding battle station, and gets back in time for an ewok party in the woods. All because of what he *decided* to do. Nobody decided it for him."

"But *Star Wars* isn't real. It's just a movie."

"*Star Wars* is not *just* a movie. It's not *just* anything." His voice was stretched so tight, it shook. "The point is, there was no stupid destiny standing in his way. The way things are is the way things are. You're all alone on this mountain, and I have these legs, and that's it." He balled his hands into fists. "That's it. No offense."

My cheeks burned. "You don't know what you're talking about." I tried to keep my voice steady. "And it's not stupid." I had dug up everything that was buried inside me and left it there on the ground in front of him. And he was stomping on it.

"All I'm saying is that I've found a lot of different stuff on digs with my pop, and none of it has ever been somebody's destiny. It sounds pretty impossible."

He was right. It did. But I believed in impossible things.

"But the fortune said—"

"Can I see it?" Galen asked. "Can I see the fortune?"

I dug the slip of paper out of my pocket. "All right, but prepare yourself."

"Prepare myself for what?"

"You'll see," I told him, and I handed it over.

He held the ends of the fortune between his fingers. He shrugged.

"You have to touch the letters," I said.

He pressed his thumbs over the words. "Nope."

I took it back from him and squeezed it tight in my hand. Murderation! I couldn't feel the heartbeat either. I pressed harder and, after a few very long seconds, I felt it. But it was so weak.

Don't lose heart. Don't lose heart. I buried the fortune into the deepest corner of my pocket. The circle of light from my flashlight broke away from his.

"It's just, no offense, but it seems like you're making this story up like I did with the badgers."

"I am not making it up," I said, turning to face him.

"I just don't see how someone can bury destiny."

"You can bury the past," I said. "Isn't that what archaeologists dig up? If you can bury the past, why can't you bury the future?"

"Because destiny isn't real," he said. "And even if it was, which it isn't, it's not like you could put it in a hole. Destiny is an idea. You can't bury ideas."

That wasn't true. Sometimes it felt like there was a hole inside of me where I buried lots of ideas—about my parents, about Horace, about myself. Besides, destiny was more than an idea.

I felt the anger churning in my stomach. "Give me a trinket."

"A what?" he asked.

"One of the things you brought," I told him. "The paper clip. Give me the paper clip."

He fished around in his pocket and brought up the paper clip, the silver button, and the piece of green bottle glass. I took the paper clip from him and held it above my head. "Claude!" I yelled. "I have something for you!"

"What are you doing?" Galen asked, backing away from me.

I called for Claude again.

"I'm serious, what are you—"

After a few moments, I could hear their wingbeats. They weren't there and then they were, just that quick. Claude landed in the grass off to my side. The four others in his flock flew low and circled around my head.

I could see in Galen's face that he now knew what I told him was not made up. Birds, fortune, curse, destiny. All of it was true. He believed me.

It was a satisfying thing to be believed.

I bent down to Claude and held out the paper clip to him. "Don't you want this?"

He wouldn't take it from me. He tucked his legs underneath him and flattened his body in the grass.

"What's wrong?" I asked him.

He looked at me with his one eye.

"Right," I whispered. "Stop asking questions."

"I have a question," said Galen. "Can you understand them?"

The raven who brought me Mr. Pitts's nose, the one with blue eyes, came closer to me. It looked at me like it wanted me to know something. I didn't know what. Gently, it took the paper clip with its beak.

"Only sometimes," I answered Galen. "The memories in the trinkets they give me tell me things."

Galen dropped his backpack. He fingered the silver button and the piece of green glass in his open hand. "Why do they want this stuff?"

"I'm not sure," I said. "Claude seems to like shiny things."

"Is that one Claude?" asked Galen, pointing to the raven with blue eyes, who had dropped the paper clip and was pecking at it in the grass.

"No, he's this one." I reached out to the one-eyed raven. He was very still. "But something's wrong. He's usually really interested in taking things from me."

Galen knelt beside me and Claude. He held out the button and green glass in his hand. Claude turned his head to look, but he did not take them. "Maybe he's sick?"

Before I could answer, Claude gave out a loud screech and flew at Galen, his wings beating the air like a drum. Galen screamed. He covered his face with his hands. The silver button and green glass fell to the ground.

"What's going on, Cutie?"

"I don't know!"

Then Claude flew at Galen's backpack. He took hold of the twine on the zipper pull with his beak.

"Hey!" yelled Galen. "That's mine!" He threw himself onto his backpack. "Cutie, tell him to stop! He wants my backpack!"

I shouted at Claude to stop.

Claude didn't listen.

I grabbed an end of the backpack to help Galen. And that's when I realized that Claude didn't want the backpack. He wanted the silver anchor pendant that hung from the zipper pull.

Galen must've realized it too, at the same time, because he yelled, "Get your beak off my anchor! I found it, and it's mine!"

Claude let go. He fell onto his side in the grass.

Right then, I remembered where I had seen that anchor before.

It was in the memory inside of the fortune.

The anchor was a button. On my mama's raincoat.

The day she went to Charlie's house.

I'd thought this brilliant object was lost forever! The curse makes it difficult to keep track of such things.

Carrying my collection wherever we fly is not at all practical. Or possible. Instead, I've kept it in a nest at the top of a hemlock on Smite Mountain. But my flock and I are not free to come and go to the mountain by our own will. And over the years, the nest has become weathered. Occupied by others. So many of my objects gone.

I suspect crows. The petty thieves.

The curse compels us here to witness its magic and collect a soul. Afterward, we cannot return until the next full moon rises on the solstice.

Sometimes it is a few years between occurrences.

Sometimes it is decades.

We too live at the mercy of this dreadful curse, and so much has been lost.

I grew up on this mountain. It is as much a part of me as my feathers. My beak. My one eye.

I know the trees here as well as I know anything. The air too. The way it smells.

And I don't mean the molasses.

You might think a bird could make a home anywhere, and you wouldn't be wrong exactly. But you wouldn't be right either.

This mountain is my only true home.

My, this boy is stronger than he appears. He holds tight to what he thinks belongs to him. I can respect that.

The shine on the anchor has faded since I saw it last.

I do hope the memory inside hasn't.

For this memory is not mine. It is Magda's.

CHAPTER 26

I TRIED TO PRY GALEN'S FINGERS OFF THE ANCHOR. I NEEDED TO HOLD the button in my hand and see what it had to show me about my mama. I needed to find out what had happened to her.

"What are you doing, Cutie?" Galen asked, tightening his grip.

I was on my knees next to him. "Let go," I told him.

"No," he said. "The bird will take it!"

"He won't," I told him, pulling at his hands. "There's something inside it that Claude wants me to see!"

Galen let go then, but I could tell he didn't want to.

I looked at Claude. He was so still, lying there in the grass. I didn't know if he was alive or not. But before I could check on him, the jolt of electricity from the memory shot through me and went right to my heart.

The first thing I saw, when Claude and Galen faded away, was the moon. It was perfectly round and glowing. It looked lonely up there in the dark sky, all by itself. And then, as other things came into focus, I saw Horace. He was a boy, and he was running hard down the mountain.

He had the rifle in his hand.

As he got closer to the farmhouse, I saw the wooden door to the root cellar set into a steep hill.

Horace jumped off the hill and landed in front of the door. His knees buckled, and he stumbled in the grass. Right into Charlie. Charlie was young, but I recognized his sharp chin and lizard face right away. In one shove, Charlie knocked Horace to the ground. Horace rolled to a stop and let go of the rifle. He yelled out in pain.

Charlie stood over him and shined a kerosene lantern in his face. "Surprise, dummy," he said.

"Charlie?" Horace said, panting. "What are you doing here?"

"Spotlighting deer along the creek. Got two doe and a six-point buck with a bow and arrow. Heard a gunshot and wanted to see who else was on the mountain."

"Spotlighting deer is illegal," Horace said, wincing as he got to his feet.

Charlie stepped in front of him. "What, you gonna turn me in, dummy? Besides, I wanna know what you're doin' out here."

Horace tried to push past Charlie. "I need to get home."

Charlie blocked his path. "That wasn't you I heard, was it? You weren't out here shooting, were you? Nah, what am I sayin'? You ain't got it in you."

Horace glanced at his rifle lying on the ground a few feet away.

Charlie saw it too. "Or do you?"

Horace scrambled to his rifle and picked it up. "I said I've got to go home."

"No way," Charlie said, grabbing hold of Horace's shirt with his fist and pushing him up against the root-cellar door. "I'm not leaving until you tell me what you shot."

Horace struggled against the weight of Charlie, who was at least a head taller than him and twice as wide.

While Horace and Charlie tussled, I saw something move behind a row of mountain fetterbushes at the bottom of the slope. I got closer and saw that my mama was hiding there. Watching. She was wearing the raincoat with the anchor buttons.

"Fine," Horace said, breaking free of Charlie's hold. "A bird. I shot a bird, okay?" He wiped at his eyes.

So this was the same night that Horace shot out Claude's eye. I thought it would be the memory of what happened when Mama took the box from Charlie's house. I thought it would show me what happened to her.

Charlie slapped his knee and grinned.

"A bird? A bird! Man oh day, I figured it would be small like a fox or coon or something. But a bird. That takes the cake, Horace. You killed an itty-bitty bird! What a weakling you are!"

Horace swore and wiped his eyes with his shirt-sleeve. "It's not dead," Horace spit out. "It's hurt. Its eye . . . it's pretty bad, I think." He closed his eyes.

Charlie shrugged. "Show me. I wanna see it."

Horace opened his eyes and shook his head. "No."

Charlie grabbed Horace's arm and gave him a shove up the mountain. "I said, show me."

The mountain was draped in mist. It swirled like ghosts as they climbed. Every now and then, Horace slowed his steps, and Charlie gave him another shove.

I followed alongside my mama. The closer we got to where I knew Claude was, the tighter the knots pulled inside me.

When Charlie and Horace found Claude, the five ravens in his flock were in a circle around him. The birds puffed up their chests, flicked their tails, and screeched at the two boys.

Mama stopped at a hawthorn shrub and hid behind it.

"There," Horace said, pointing at Claude. He kept a distance and looked away.

Charlie took a step closer and held up his kerosene lantern. "You got its eye, that ain't half bad."

Claude's flock stretched out their wings and screamed at Charlie and Horace.

My heart was pounding in my ears. Horace gasped and clutched his chest as if the screams pierced him through.

"Come on, let's go," Horace begged. His body was shaking. "It's got to be nearly midnight. I need—I need . . . to get home."

"Give me that," Charlie said, nodding in the direction of the rifle.

"What?" Horace asked.

"Your gun," Charlie said. "Give it to me."

Claude tried to stand, but he couldn't find his footing. I stepped closer to him. *He lives,* I reminded myself. *Claude's going to be all right. The other ravens too. They're going to be all right.*

"Look," Horace said, gripping the barrel of his rifle tight. "I don't want this."

"This is the last time I'm gonna say it," said Charlie, stepping closer to Horace. "Give me your gun."

"Don't do it!" I yelled at Horace. "Don't!"

But nobody in the memory heard me.

Horace lowered his head. He loosened his hold. He reached out his arm.

And then he let go.

Charlie grabbed the rifle from him and aimed at Horace, who was standing between him and the birds. "Now move," he said to Horace.

No, no, no.

Horace looked like he was trying to decide what to do. Like he was faced with an impossible choice. Standing there, in that spot, on the mountain, Horace seemed as alone as that moon.

I ran to the hawthorn shrub where my mama was watching. I wanted her to do something. To help Horace. To help Claude. But at the same time, I wanted her to stay hidden so she'd be safe.

"I'm not going to say it again," said Charlie, his lizard face staring down the barrel of the rifle. "Move!"

And so, Horace did.

I forced my eyes shut. I didn't want to see.

I pressed my hands tighter and tighter against my ears, but the blasts of the rifle were too loud, too horrible, and too close to shut out. "Stop! Stop, please, please stop!" I screamed. The blasts went on and on. I couldn't make them stop.

I opened my eyes for just a second or two and saw

Charlie shooting straight into the trees. He was grinning. The whole time, he was grinning.

When he finally stopped, the quiet that came after was just about worse. There was nothing. A hollowed-out emptiness that made the hair on my arms stand up.

I opened my eyes and uncovered my ears. I saw Charlie standing over the birds. The rifle was still in his grip.

I moved past Charlie and knelt next to Claude. He was the only one of his flock left alive. Claude lifted his head and tried to get to his feet.

"Why? Why would you do that?" I hollered, even though I knew Charlie couldn't hear me.

He stepped away from the birds then. He knelt next to branches on the ground. I followed him. That's when I saw the nest. Chunks of it were scattered all around. Sticks caked with mud, woven grass, strips of bark. Feathers. Leaves. Broken eggs.

They had a nest. And eggs.

Charlie sifted through the sticks and feathers. He stopped when he saw it: an unbroken egg. It was nestled in a chunk of woven grass and leaves. The egg was pale blue-green with brown specks and swirls. It was a beautiful thing. A beautiful, whole thing, when everything around it was in pieces.

"Hoo boy," Charlie said. He picked up the egg and held it in his hand. Then he stuffed it into the pocket of his jacket.

Horace stood there silent. Like always, he just let Charlie take whatever he wanted.

Then I heard a soft whistle. It was coming from the tops of the trees. Or maybe higher than the trees. Maybe it was coming from the moon.

Horace and Charlie heard it too. They looked up.

I couldn't see anything but the moon.

The whistle grew into a roar. It was coming closer.

The wind gusted, bending branches. It whooshed past what was left of the nest, stirring the woven sticks, grass, and broken eggs. Then it blew over Claude's flock, pausing at each raven before moving on to the next, like it was sniffing out what had just happened. It swirled around Claude last and lifted him to his feet.

Horace and Charlie backed up.

The wind left Claude and churned around Horace's legs. His T-shirt caught the air and ballooned at the hem.

Charlie was still while the wind sized him up. The flap of his jacket pocket fluttered open in the air. The same pocket where he had put the egg. It looked like the wind was trying to get into that pocket, and maybe Charlie thought that too, because real carefully, he slipped his hand into his pocket and kept it there.

I don't know if the wind gave up then, but it left Charlie alone and then in one strong blast, it set upon Horace and struck him down.

CHAPTER
27

IT FELT LIKE THE GROUND WAS SHAKING. ALL AROUND ME, IT FELT like an earthquake. I got to my feet. Galen was looking at me funny. "Are you okay?" he asked. But I could barely hear him. He seemed so far away.

Then I realized, an earthquake wasn't happening around me. It was happening inside me. I was trembling. *If a butterfly in Texas could cause a hurricane on the other side of the world, could seeing something that happened so long ago cause an earthquake inside me?*

I heard my name. It was soft at first. Then louder. *Cutie. Hey, Cutie?*

It was like a string dangling in the dark. I grabbed hold of it tight. Until the darkness started to fade and the earth stopped quaking. And there was Galen. "Are you okay?" he asked again.

I looked at him. "I don't know."

The raven with blue eyes flew to my shoulder. It let out some low croaking sounds and gently pecked at my hair. I held very still. Slowly, I reached up and touched its neck. It was the softest thing I'd ever felt.

Next to Galen, Claude puffed his chest.

Galen said, "Cutie, I'm not sure what just happened, but whatever you tell me, I promise you I will one hundred percent believe it."

I stopped petting the raven, and it stayed on my shoulder. I could feel its strong feet holding on to me. "I know what started the curse."

"What?" Galen asked.

I told Galen about the memory inside the anchor button and what Charlie did to those birds. And how the curse was set on Horace, and that's why every time there was a full moon on the summer solstice, someone in Horace's family was taken away. Someone in *my* family. "But there's one thing I don't understand," I said.

"Only one thing?" Galen said, shaking his head. "You're way ahead of me."

"Charlie was the one who did it," I said. "Horace had a hand in it, I know. But Charlie is the one who killed those birds. If there's anyone who should have a curse set on him, it's Charlie!"

Galen nodded.

"Why is Charlie so worried about the curse if it's not set on him?" I said. "Why is he trying so hard to find what's buried by the weeping willow?"

"Maybe Charlie doesn't know that the birds cursed Horace and not him," Galen said.

"Maybe," I said. "Or maybe he is protected from the curse somehow."

"How would he be protected from a curse?"

"I have no idea," I admitted. "But in the memory, the wind checked out Charlie and Horace, and then it left Charlie alone."

"The wind checked out Charlie and Horace?"

"I don't know if it was the wind exactly, but something came down from the moon, I think, and it whistled and blew all around like it was trying to figure out who was responsible. I know it all sounds like some fairy story, like I'm making it up."

"Yeah, it does." Galen looked at the raven perched

on my shoulder. "But that doesn't mean I don't believe you."

Then the raven flew off my shoulder and landed next to Claude and the others.

I held out my hand to Galen, and I was surprised when he grabbed it and let me help him up. He pulled on his backpack, and I handed him the anchor button.

"It's okay," he said, "you can have it."

I wasn't sure that I really wanted it after seeing the awful memory inside it. But now that I had a collection of things going, it felt like each was a piece of a story that the birds were telling me. And this anchor was a big piece. I thanked him and shoved it into my pocket.

"Ready?" Galen asked.

Claude tried to fly, but he barely got any air before he hit the ground again. I went over to him and pulled some grass out of the ground. "You stay here, okay?" I said, piling the grass around Claude's body for a soft nest. "We're going to dig up my destiny, and that will break the curse. I'll come back for you. All right?"

Claude let out a sigh and lowered his head.

"I know, I know, stop asking questions," I said. "But I'll take that as a yes."

I pulled the map out of my pocket. I told Galen I was ready. And then we headed east to find the willow.

The girl won't have the opportunity to come back for me.
But her intentions are appreciated.

This girl.

I still haven't looked into her heart. But even so, I
know that I was wrong before. She is different than most
humans I've encountered.

This is what I know about most humans:

Humans are pathetically slow.

And predictable.

They charge at you with brooms or shovels. And some-
times guns.

They are untrustworthy.

It's their stupidity that makes them untrustworthy,

and because they're untrustworthy, they do the worst things.

There was a time when I believed Horace deserved this curse. That it was a fair price for what he and Charlie did. But I was wrong about that too.

So many have paid for it. This girl certainly has.

She may have paid the highest price of all.

I've shown her so much. About the curse. And what happened to her family.

And yet.

There is one thing she still does not know.

One thing that I cannot show her.

CHAPTER 28

"WHAT DO YOU THINK IS WRONG WITH HIM?" I ASKED GALEN, WHEN we were a good ways from where we left the ravens.

"Who?"

"Claude."

"Oh. I don't know," Galen said. "He didn't look like he was injured or anything. I don't know how long ravens live, but he's got to be really old if your uncle shot out his eye when he was a kid."

"Yeah." That was probably it, Claude was just old. But still, I was worried. What if it had something to do with the curse? "How much farther is it to where the house was?" I asked. It was dark under the canopy, and the trees kept me from seeing the moon.

"After we get through these trees," Galen said, "there's a clearing, and then it's just over a hill."

Don't lose heart, I told myself. *Don't lose heart.*

"Do you have names for the other ravens?" Galen asked.

"No," I said. "Claude seems to be the leader of the flock. He's the one that brought me all the memories. Except for the raven with the blue eyes. It brought me the nose."

"You know a group of ravens isn't called a flock?" Galen said. "It's called an unkindness."

An unkindness of ravens. That didn't seem to fit.

"There's also a confusion of guinea fowl, a parliament of owls, a murmuration of starlings, and my personal favorite, a murder of crows. My mom got me a book once on collective nouns that nobody uses. Want to know what a group of badgers is called?"

"An unkindness of ravens," I repeated. "Why is it called that?"

Galen shrugged. "I think because they're really protective of their territory. They work together to drive out other predators so they can steal their food. My pop was really into bird-watching a couple of years ago, and we visited the Cornell Lab of Ornithology. It's a place that studies birds. They're really smart, though, ravens. They play games like keep-away with pinecones and sticks, and sometimes they'll taunt other animals."

They did that with my chokecherries, I thought. But still, "unkindness" felt wrong. Maybe they were misunderstood. Maybe they were just trying to get by.

Up until that point, the forest floor had been pretty flat, but here it was thick with gnarled roots that stuck up all over. It slowed our steps.

"Sometimes they're also called a storytelling of ravens," Galen said.

A storytelling. "That suits them better." I reached into my pocket and pulled out the fortune. I pressed my fingers over the words. The heartbeat was slow. It seemed very, very far away.

Galen saw me holding the fortune. "What's wrong?"

"The heartbeat," I said. "It's barely there."

"Whose heartbeat do you think it is?"

I didn't answer right away. It was a hard thing to say out loud because I wanted it to be true. There was nothing in the whole universe I wanted more. "It's my mama's," I told him. "I think she's out there somewhere, and when I break the curse, she's going to come back."

Galen didn't say anything. But that was all right by me because I'd rather him say nothing than say that it was impossible.

We came out of the woods into a wide field. The moon was waiting for me.

"There," Galen said.

"I see it." The moon was just above the treetops. It was big and pinkish orange. It looked close enough that I could reach out and touch it. "The Rose Moon."

"No, I mean *there*." Galen was pointing toward a field. "See those stones over there by that hillside? That's the old root cellar where I found the map. The foundation for the house is just across the way."

We took off into the field. I swept my flashlight back and forth. When we got about halfway across, my flashlight caught the shadow of something off to the right. Whatever it was moved. "Hold on," I said, motioning for Galen to stop.

From behind me, Galen whispered, "What's the matter?"

I shifted my flashlight, training the light along the edge of the tall grass. The round light took in low-flying moths, fireflies, and then two thin legs.

I raised my flashlight higher. Murderation! Standing there, under the full Rose Moon, was Horace.

I stuffed the map underneath my shirt. Then I pressed my body into the ground and tried to make myself small. *A baby mouse, a walnut, a kernel of corn, a grain of wheat, a piece of dirt, a speck of dust. A baby mouse, a walnut, a kernel of corn* . . . If Horace was out here in the middle of the night, Charlie was with him. Moments later, I heard footsteps. I felt the ground underneath me tremble. Then a light trained on my face.

"Cutie," Horace said.

I squinted up at him, but the light was so bright in my eyes, I couldn't see his face.

"Well, look at what we have here," said a voice I knew belonged to Charlie.

I stared at the laces on their big boots, which were inches from my face. Horace's were pulled so tight across his giant feet that they had become thin in places, as if they were having a hard time keeping him contained. Next to Charlie's boots was the blade of a shovel. Its pointed tip burrowed into the dirt as Charlie rolled the long, wooden handle in his fingers.

I got to my knees. The map shifted under my shirt and scratched at my skin. I tried my hardest to ignore it.

"What are you doing out here in the dark, girlie?" Charlie asked. His voice was raspy and low but also playful, in the way that a fox might talk to a chicken. "There are lots of things that can happen to little girlies out here in the woods." He winked at me and smiled. Then he spat tobacco juice out of the side of his mouth. It landed in the grass next to me, but I caught some of the spray on my arm.

My cheeks burned. There was a feeling bubbling up inside me. *Is it fear? Or something else?* "I should ask you the same," I squeaked out. "Digging for treasure?"

Horace moved his lantern to his side, and I could see him better. His face was pale, and he looked so tired. He fixed his eyes on me but seemed to look through me. "What do you know of a treasure that might be out here?" he said.

"I don't."

"She does too," Charlie said. "I told you she knew

where it was hidden. She's been working with those birds."

"I don't even know what you're talking about," I said.

"Liar," Charlie said, narrowing his eyes at me. "If you don't know so much, then what are you doing all the way down here so late at night?"

I tried to think of a reason, but I wasn't fast enough.

"I'll tell you," Galen answered.

I had forgotten about Galen. I looked behind me, and there he was, flat on his stomach with his chin resting in the dirt. Had he fallen? Or was he on the ground because I was? I shook my head at him, hoping that he would see me and stop talking.

"Look," Charlie said, shining his flashlight at Galen. "Girlie brought a friend."

Galen slowly got to his feet.

"An itty-bitty friend," Charlie said, and I wished I had a rock to throw at him.

"Good one," Galen said quietly, shaking his head. Then he cleared his throat. "We know what you're looking for."

What is he doing?

Horace took one giant stride and was next to him. The wind lifted my hair as he passed. "What did you say?"

Next to Galen, Horace was a giant.

I started for them, but Charlie caught me with the handle of the shovel. He pulled me in front of him and trapped me against him with the shovel across my stomach. I wriggled to try to get loose, but Charlie tightened his grip.

"Girlie, you better answer the question," Charlie said. "Tell me what you know."

My heart was crashing inside my chest. I tried to make myself small, but with Charlie so close and his breath smelling like chewing tobacco, the only part of me that got small was my voice. "I know about the curse," I said. "I know what you did. That awful, terrible thing."

"You know less than squat," Charlie said. "You're just like your mother. That magpie tried to take what wasn't hers. It didn't end so good for her either."

"My mama tried to end the curse!" I said, pushing against the shovel handle.

Horace groaned. "Magda. My Blue Angel."

"She wanted to undo the curse, Uncle Horace."

"Grandma Pearlie Mae. Mother. Pa." Horace's voice was ragged. "They're all gone because of me."

"There's still time," I said. "I'm going to make things right. And I'm going to bring my mama back. I'm going to bring them *all* back."

"There ain't no bringing any of them back," Charlie growled. "Not from what they became, what they are now."

"How do you know?" Galen yelled.

Horace put his shaky hand on Galen's shoulder and told him to be quiet.

"There ain't no bringing them back," Charlie said. "Because what they became is birds."

"Charlie, don't," Horace whispered.

"What are you talking about?" I asked.

"Horace never did tell you?" Charlie said. "Well, you ain't much for figuring then, are you, girlie? There were six ravens that night Horace and I went up the mountain. The one-eyed bird and five others. I took care of the five. But every time there's a full moon on the longest day, those birds have come back, and when they do, they've got another one in their flock."

"Technically," Galen said, "a group of ravens isn't a flock, it's a—"

"That doesn't mean anything," I said to Charlie. "There are lots of ravens in the world. Maybe they join new flocks all the time."

Charlie chewed his tobacco. His face was so close to mine, I could hear the juice slurp in his mouth. "Go on, Horace," Charlie demanded. "Tell her what you saw."

Horace was staring up at the moon.

"I said tell her," Charlie snapped. He pulled the shovel handle toward him, and I could feel the map under my shirt pressing into my stomach.

Horace looked as fragile as Mr. Pitts. I imagined cracks running all through him.

"Tell me," I said to Horace, before he broke into a thousand pieces. "For once, just tell me something."

Horace looked at me. He craned his neck and blinked his eyes a couple of times like he just noticed I was there. "Cutie?" he said. "You shouldn't be here. You shouldn't be a part of this."

"I *am* a part of this. So please, just tell me what you saw."

He swallowed. Then he opened his mouth and

closed it. He waited for the words to come. "Some years after Grandma Pearlie Mae, there was another full moon on the solstice." He talked slowly, and it looked like it took some effort. "Me and Magda, we were helping Mother at the Solstice Festival. I was running the silent auction. Magda, she was over at the dunking booth. There were games late into the night. Music. I remember the music. And dancing. Mother, she was making a speech. The last speech of the festival, just before midnight. To welcome summer." He sniffed and ran his tongue over his dry lips. "Two ravens were there in a tree next to the stage. I seen them. The raven that I shot . . . the one missing an . . ."

"The raven that's missing an eye," I said, finishing for him.

He nodded. "And another one." He grimaced. "The full moon was out, and one second Mother was talking to the crowd, finishing her speech, and the next a wild pitch from the dunking booth flew at the stage. The ball hit Mother here." Horace raised his trembling hand and pointed to his forehead. "It came out of nowhere, and she was . . . she was gone. Right in front of my eyes. She was gone, and when I looked up, the two ravens in that tree had become three."

What is he saying? That at midnight, his mother died and disappeared? And she turned into a bird? "That can't be."

"There's lots of things that can't be that are," Charlie said. He tightened the shovel against me. "Go on. Tell her the rest, Horace."

Horace wiped his eyes with his T-shirt. "Nine years later it was Pa's turn. He'd been sleeping out in his workshop for years, ever since . . . Couldn't stand being in the house with Mother gone. So that night, when the full moon came again on the solstice, Pa was asleep in his Studebaker. Blasted, he loved that car more than he loved . . ." His voice trailed off. "Midnight came 'round, and then. A sinkhole. That's what got him. Swallowed him and the car. His whole workshop. Everything. There were four ravens after that." Horace dropped to his knees.

Four ravens. But why? Why would they become birds? I thought about what I'd seen in the memory the night Charlie shot those birds. How the wind blew over each of the birds lying there, like it was trying to make out what had happened to them. And how it checked out Charlie and Horace. To find out who was responsible.

If Horace was telling the truth, and a new raven showed up every time the curse took someone, did that mean the curse was going to replace Claude's flock, all those ravens Charlie shot?

When the birds brought me something, they took something in return. One for one.

Pearlie Mae, Horace's mother, and Horace's pa. That's three.

"Plus Claude makes four. And Magda would be . . . she would be . . . five." As soon as I said the words, I knew that the raven with the blue eyes was my mama. "No. No. No!"

Horace choked out, "My Blue Angel."

"Now they're back for one more," Charlie said.

The knots inside of me pulled so tight, they burned. Charlie had caused all this to happen. He was the reason my mama was gone. He was the reason I never had the chance to know her. I pushed hard against Charlie, which must've taken him by surprise, because he loosened his hold on the shovel. I got free of his grip. At the same time, the map that was under my shirt slid out and onto the ground.

"What's this?" Charlie asked, beating me to it. He

snatched it up with one hand. "I told you she knew where it was, Horace. You dummy. I told you she had it all along."

"Give it back!" Galen yelled.

"Give it back!" Charlie said, mimicking Galen's voice.

I tried to grab the map, but Charlie shoved me down.

"I'm going to get back what was mine," he said. "And when the curse strikes again, I'll be protected"—he pointed to himself—"and one of you will be a bird. I think that's what they call killing two birds with one stone."

Then I heard wingbeats behind me. Followed by high-pitched screeches. I got to my feet real quick and looked into the night sky. They were impossible to see in the dark, until they were on top of us. I ducked when the ravens dove at Horace and Charlie.

I stomped on Charlie's boot as hard as I could, grabbed the map from him, and shouted at Galen, "Run!"

CHAPTER 29

WE RAN SOUTH, OUT OF THE FIELD AND ACROSS THE CREEK. Galen kept up for a while, longer than I thought he might, but he fell behind once we got past the tree line. "Slow down," he called, huffing.

I stopped at an elm and waited for him to catch up. Horace's lantern light was bobbing in the dark not far behind him. "We need to get moving."

"I'm not going to make it, Cutie," Galen said. "Maybe you should go on by yourself."

"No way. I'm not leaving you here. Come on." I handed him the map. Then I swung his arm over my shoulder and tried to half carry him. The tree roots on top of the ground were like a tangle of long fingers that tried to trip us every which way. They were aiming to bring us down. I led Galen around them as best as I could, but then a mess of fallen branches snagged at our clothes.

"You can't get away," Charlie taunted from somewhere close. His voice made a shiver scuttle up my neck.

"It's no use," Galen whispered. His grip on my shoulder tightened, and he pulled me to a stop.

I switched off my flashlight, and Galen did the same. We crouched behind the trunk of an elm. If we were small enough, maybe Charlie and Horace would pass us by. Or maybe Claude and his flock would find us and help us.

If Claude and the others were still out there. If Horace and Charlie hadn't hurt them, or worse.

It wasn't long before we heard heavy boots snapping twigs and crushing undergrowth. The sounds got closer. Louder. My heart pounded wildly in my ears. The light from Horace's lantern swept across the tree trunks on our left, and then on the forest floor beside us. I could smell the stink of Charlie's tobacco chew.

"They're close by, I can feel it," Charlie said. "Shine your light over there."

I held my breath. I told myself over and over to be small. But the edge of his light caught the map in Galen's hand.

I heard Horace gasp.

Then a snap of a twig farther away. "Over here," yelled Charlie. "This way."

Horace mumbled something I couldn't make out, and then his light swung away from us, followed by his bootsteps.

I leaned forward and watched their light get smaller as they moved farther away from us, heading deeper into the woods. When I couldn't see Horace's light anymore, I got to my feet.

"I thought for sure he saw us," Galen whispered, pulling himself up.

"Yeah," I said. "Me too." The thing was, Horace did see us. I was sure of it. The light from his lantern landed on the map.

"I thought it was over for us back there," he said. "Good thing those birds came back."

"Do you think Claude and the flock are all right?"

Galen shrugged. "I don't know. Cutie, I'm scared."

"Me too."

It was quiet. I waited a little while longer to be safe and then said, "Come on, let's go." I switched on my flashlight and started off. We only got a few steps when a light trained on us from a few yards away.

"Gotcha!" shouted Charlie, running for us. He tripped over a tree root, landing on top of his shovel. Behind him, Horace raised his lantern close to his face. He was staring at me, and he looked afraid.

I screamed, "Go!" And Galen and I took off back toward the clearing. I knew with our flashlights on, they'd have no trouble seeing where we went, but under the dark canopy we didn't have a choice.

Branches cracked behind us. Heavy boot falls. Swearing.

"I've got an idea," I said to Galen. "Follow me."

"What do you think I've been doing?" he asked, breathing hard.

We were almost to the clearing when I looked back and saw Charlie and Horace gaining on us. Then I slowed down until Galen was beside me.

"Horace," hollered Charlie, "get up here with that lantern. I've almost got 'em!"

"What are you doing?" Galen asked. "They're right behind us."

I grabbed Galen's arm. "On the count of three," I whispered, "switch off your flashlight."

"What for?"

"Just do it, okay? One . . ." I stole another glance behind me. Charlie was just a few yards from us, and Horace wasn't far behind him. His lantern was swinging as he stumbled around the trees.

"Horace!" yelled Charlie. "Hurry up! I can hardly see!"

"Two . . ." I said, gripping Galen's arm tight. We were almost there. I swung my flashlight to the right to see what would be in our path. There was a cluster of pines, but beyond that, an opening into the clearing.

Galen said, "Cutie, watch out, we're headed right for—"

"Three!" Galen and I shut off our flashlights as I yanked his arm to the right and kept on going, feeling my way past the pines in the dark.

"Yeeoooooow!" came from behind us. With the sudden darkness in front of him, there was no way for Charlie to see the spiky thorns of the honey locust in his path. And like I hoped, he ran right into them.

CHAPTER 30

W E DIDN'T STOP RUNNING UNTIL WE REACHED THE CLEARING. THE moon was right above us. I let go of Galen's arm and switched on my flashlight. Beads of sweat were dripping down the side of Galen's face, and he was panting hard. "Was that—"

"Honey locust," I told him, trying to catch my breath.

"Ouch," he said. "Genius. But, ouch."

Galen pulled the map from his pocket and pointed his flashlight at it. "We're back in the clearing," he said, looking around. He tapped the drawing of the house on the map. "Which means the house should be just south of us."

I traced the dotted lines from the back of the house, across the creek, and to the weeping willow with my finger. "What time is it?"

"Ten fourteen," Galen said.

Another yell came from the direction of the honey locust. "We've got a little more than an hour," I said. "Let's go." I shut off my flashlight. "We'll need to keep our flashlights off as long as we can."

We ran across the clearing until Galen said he couldn't run anymore, and then we walked. But we kept on moving.

We hugged the tree line until we found where the house used to be. The forest had swallowed it up. All that was left was a stone foundation and a brick chimney stack. A few charred timbers. They were peeking out through an overgrowth of thick brush and brambles.

I stopped and tried to picture what the house looked like in the memories. The wide porch. The tall shutters. Ten years ago, my mama and I lived here. And Uncle Horace too. It was almost impossible to believe how one thing that had happened so long ago—one awful, terrible thing—could take away so much.

It was just like Toot had said: *Everything in this world comes with a price. Somebody always has to pay.*

We crossed the creek, following the line on the map, and headed back into the woods. When we were deep under the thick canopy of the forest, and out of the moonlight, we switched our flashlights back on.

The woods didn't seem interested in what Galen and I were up to and went on about their usual business.

The fireflies played hide-and-seek.

An owl asked a question.

A luna moth glided past us, looking for a mate.

We were quiet for the longest time. *They became birds. Birds.* That's what I was thinking. I could think of nothing else. I had been with them. Yelled at them for stealing my chokecherries. Wished for an asteroid. Fed them circus peanuts.

My great-grandma Pearlie Mae. My grandparents. My mama.

Birds.

But why didn't they come before now? Where have they been all this time?

There must've been a reason for them to stay away. There's been a reason for everything else they've done.

I thought about how the raven with blue eyes—my mama—had sat on my shoulder. How she pecked at my hair. How soft her feathers felt.

The flutter in my heart came back again. It lasted a long time.

They can come back, I told myself. *Even if they're birds. Breaking the curse will bring them back. Won't it?*

"What do you know about curse breaking?" I asked Galen.

"Nothing. Unless you count from stories," he said. "My mom used to read me fairy tales when I was little. There were always lots of curses being broken in them. Mostly by kissing a prince. They're the worst. I made my mom skip over that part." He adjusted his backpack on his shoulders. "There's one story where a man was turned into a tree by a curse from an old witch. And he was freed by a young servant girl when she found a ring. There's another one where this father sent his seven sons out to fetch some water for their young sister, who was sick, and when they returned without any water, the father cursed them. He turned them into ravens." He nudged me with his elbow. "Hey, ravens. I just remembered that part."

"What happened?"

"I forgot a lot of it, but there's something about a chicken bone that their sister loses, and so she has to chop off her finger to unlock the Glass Mountain. Which she does, and the ravens turn back into her brothers, and she brings them home."

"They turn back into her brothers?" I repeated, hopeful. "Okay."

He shined his flashlight on my fingers.

"What?" I said.

"Just checking to see which finger we might need to unlock the Glass Mountain."

"Very funny," I said. But it really wasn't.

"When we find what's buried by the weeping willow, do you think the curse will automatically be broken?" Galen asked. "Or do you have to do something else?"

"I don't know," I admitted. "The fortune says 'Uncover your destiny, and you will remake history.' Once we uncover it, everything should go back to the way it's supposed to be." The truth was, I wasn't sure. "Maybe Claude will tell me if I need to do something else. If Claude's all right. Did you see how many ravens came when we were with Horace and Charlie?"

Galen shook his head. "It was too dark, and it happened really fast. Why's he called Claude again?"

"I named him," I said. "After Claude Monet. The painter."

"The bird paints too?" asked Galen. He was about to step in a groundhog hole.

"Watch out." I grabbed his arm and pulled him around it.

"Thanks. That could've been bad," he said, looking back into the hole. "Hey, you know what? I just realized something. You're like Luke Skywalker. You're the chosen one who's going to bring balance back into the world."

"Uh-huh."

"I mean, except for the fact that Luke got to train with Yoda and learn how to move things with his mind. And have cool light-saber battles and blow up the Death Star. Twice. And you, well, you get to end a curse, find your family, and stop someone else from turning into a bird. So pretty much the same thing."

I pushed through a cluster of dense bittersweet. "Am I the only one looking for a weeping willow here? I mean, you know what it looks like, right?"

Galen said, "No. But if I had to guess, I'd say tall, sad, and weepy. Also willowy. Kind of like that one over there." He pointed his flashlight to the left.

I looked in the direction of his light, and there it was. A weeping willow. It had long, drooping branches. Like a hundred sagging shoulders.

The tree looked forgotten.

But at the same time, beautiful. And hopeful. Like it believed one day someone would remember it was there. And when that day came, the tree would straighten its shoulders and be ready to help.

Galen pulled a trowel from his backpack. I grabbed a nearby rock with a sharp edge.

At the base of the tree, we started to dig.

CHAPTER 31

GALEN STABBED THE DIRT WITH HIS TROWEL. "I REALLY WISH WE had that Charlie guy's shovel."

The ground was hard, and after what seemed to be a very long time, the hole was only a few inches deep. I was using the rock to scrape out the dirt.

"Maybe you could get the birds to bring us one?" Then he shook his head. "I can't believe I just asked if *birds* could bring us a shovel."

"I don't think they could carry one," I said. "Besides, if we start hollering for Claude, Horace and Charlie will find us in a hurry."

I wiped the sweat away from my forehead. Some of the dirt that we'd piled between us slipped back into the hole. I dragged it back out again. My fingers hurt. There were gashes on my knuckles. I stopped and pressed my T-shirt against my bloodied hand. "Do you want to trade?" Galen asked, offering me his trowel.

"No thanks," I said, gripping the rock and forcing it back into the hole.

Galen kept digging. He was fast, and his arms were strong.

The hole got deeper. And emptier.

"Maybe this isn't the right spot," I said, worried.

"On the map, the box is on the west side of the tree," said Galen. "And this is the west side of the tree."

"Maybe this isn't the right willow," I said.

"Maybe," he said, pausing and catching his breath. "But I don't see another one, do you?"

I looked around, scanning the trees with my flashlight. "No."

Galen continued digging. I set the flashlight on the ground beside me, pointing it at the hole.

Galen said, "Some Indigenous people thought of the willow tree as protection, my pop says. They would carry branches with them in their canoes to protect against storms."

"Hey, look at that," I said. "You do know something about trees."

"Told you."

"Do you think that's the reason my mama chose this tree?" I had decided that since she took the box from Charlie, then she had to be the one that hid it here. And she drew the map so that I would find it. "To protect whatever's buried here?"

"Maybe," he said. "Or maybe there isn't a reason. Maybe she was just tired of walking through the woods, and when she sat down to rest her weary bones, the willow just happened to be there. There doesn't have to be a reason for everything, you know. Sometimes things just are." He stopped digging. "And sometimes they just aren't."

From someplace behind us came the crack of a branch. We froze. I fumbled my flashlight and shut it off. I grabbed for Galen's flashlight, but he had it in his hands and was shining it in the direction of the noise. "What are you doing?" I whispered. "They'll see us." But just as I said the words, a red fox stepped into the light. It paused to look at us, its eyes alert and wary, and then disappeared into the dark.

My heart was thumping, and my stomach felt sick. I took a big breath and switched my flashlight on again. Galen pointed his at the hole.

It was empty.

"What if this is just like the empty fortune cookie?" I whispered. My chest ached as I said the words.

"What do you mean?"

I told Galen about my eighth birthday when Toot took me to Darryl's All-You-Can-Eat China Buffet and Subs. And how when I opened my fortune cookie, there was no fortune inside.

We both stared at the hole. "What if there's nothing buried here?" I asked.

For once, Galen didn't have an answer.

Don't lose heart, I told myself. Then I reached into my pocket and fished out the fortune. I squeezed it tight in my hand. The heartbeat was even farther away. I was losing it. The knots inside me jerked tight.

"No," I said out loud. "It's here. It has to be." I shoved the rock into the dirt.

Galen was watching me. "Cutie—"

I didn't know exactly what he was going to say, but whatever it was, I didn't want to hear it. My hands slammed into the dirt. I laid the rock aside and clawed at the bottom of the hole with my fingers.

And then, "Ow!" My knuckles jammed against something hard. I tucked my fingers under my armpit to stop the throbbing.

"What is it?" Galen plunged his trowel into the hole and felt around the bottom. "There's something there. I mean, it could be a rock, or . . . Shine the light down there."

I grabbed my flashlight and aimed the light at Galen's hands. He worked the tip of the trowel along the side of the hole, drawing the dirt away until he could see an edge of something.

"Can you tell what it is?" My heart was racing.

"Hold on."

"But is it a rock or something else?" I leaned in closer to get a better look, but Galen's head and arms were blocking my view.

"Oh," Galen said.

"What?" I asked, hearing something in his voice. Disappointment, maybe? "It's only a rock, isn't it?"

He scooted his legs back and pushed himself out of the hole. "It's definitely not a rock." He placed something in my hands. It was a shapeless glob of dirt and tree roots, about the size of a toaster.

We pulled away chunks of caked-on dirt, letting them fall back into the hole. Soon, I could make out the thing's rectangular shape. Then its wooden corners. And then the "C" etched into the wood.

It was the box from the memory. The one my mama had found in Charlie's cabinet.

My hands shook.

"Well?" Galen said. "Open it."

"Right," I said. "Open it." I pulled at the lid, but it was stuck closed. I dug along the edge of the lid with my fingernails.

"Here." Galen handed me his trowel.

I tried again, digging the edge of the trowel around the lid and prying it loose. Then I pulled back the lid the whole way. The rusted hinges broke free of the box, and the lid fell into my lap.

Galen dropped his flashlight. "Sorry." He fumbled to pick it back up and then pointed it at the box. "Whoa. Are you serious?"

I took the pale blue-green thing out of the box and held it in my hand. "It's an egg."

CHAPTER 32

THERE WAS A MEMORY INSIDE THE EGG.

All at once, I was standing in front of Charlie's rancher. It was raining. There was a full moon behind the storm clouds.

My mama was there in her raincoat with her baby—me. She had the wooden box in her hand. She was walking toward her bicycle when Charlie appeared from around the corner of the house.

"What do you think you're doing, Magpie?" he asked, putting his hand on the bicycle seat.

My mama backed up. She cradled the box in her arm. "Taking back what doesn't belong to you."

Charlie shook his head. "You want the egg? You're

a greedy little magpie." He looked up, into the rain. The moon was a round smudge behind the clouds. "You know what's going to happen at midnight. And you're after its protection. But the egg is mine."

"You know?" my mama asked, surprised. "You've known all along that this egg kept the curse away from you, protected you? You knew it, and you just sat back and watched my family get taken? Grandma Pearlie Mae and my parents, gone. My baby's father left because he was afraid the curse was coming for him. You knew, and you could've done something to stop it."

"And let the curse get me? I don't think so."

My mama shook her head. "I saw you that night. I was there. You killed those birds! For no reason at all! *You* caused the curse! And you took everything from me!"

"It's like my daddy always told me," Charlie said, inching closer to her. "If you don't got anything, you ain't anything. Look at what that egg got me. Protection. And I kept the egg all this time to make sure I'll *always* be somebody."

"You're wrong," my mama said, taking a step backward. "You're nothing but a thief. And that makes you nothing at all."

Charlie lunged at her. My mama turned and ran. Charlie's boots slipped in the wet grass. He fell, and his nose was bloodied. Four ravens came from out of the sky and swooped at him, which gave Mama time to get to the woods.

The ravens flew until they got just ahead of her. They were making sure she was keeping up with them. But suddenly Mama changed direction and raced south.

The ravens dove and circled around her. Just like they did to me when they wanted me to follow them to Galen's campsite. They wanted her to follow them. But she didn't. Instead, she went deeper and deeper into the woods.

Go with the birds. I wanted to tell her. *They're trying to tell you how to break the curse.*

The sky broke into a downpour. The moon hid behind the clouds like it was afraid to see what was going to happen next.

Mama made it across Whistling Creek and then headed east. She was soaked and winded by the time she got to the weeping willow. The tree's waterlogged branches made a heavy curtain around its trunk. Behind the curtain, Mama found an opening. "I don't know if I can do this," she whispered to me, the baby tucked inside her raincoat. Her voice wobbled.

Not long after, he came. "Magpie!" Charlie yelled. "I know you're out here someplace. You can't hide forever. I'll find you. And I'll get that egg. You can be sure of that."

Mama stayed quiet under the protection of the tree. Her hands were trembling. I wanted so much to hold them.

The ravens called to her from the top of the willow after Charlie had gone deeper into the woods. They were trying to tell her something, maybe that it was safe to come out; I wasn't sure. She peeked from behind the willow branches. "Birds," she whispered into the storm. "Are you there?"

Rrack-rrack-rack, they answered and moved to a bough near her.

She opened the box and showed them the egg. "Here! Take it!"

Rrack-rrack-rack. They only stared at her. Claude lowered his head like he was disappointed. Like he had been counting on my mama to know what to do.

"I can't get the egg back up the mountain before midnight," Mama said. "Not without Charlie finding me. I can't! So you need to take it. Please!"

The birds got quiet.

"Why won't you help her?" I yelled at Claude and the others. "Why won't you take the egg?"

I heard Galen's voice then. He sounded so far away.

I shook my head and squeezed my eyes shut and went deeper inside the memory.

Mama looked so very tired.

Claude stretched out his wings and touched her hand. When he did, Mama got a scared, knowing look in her eyes. Something had passed between them.

"Horace," she whispered. "It all started with Horace and Charlie. It has to end with them."

Then Claude flew into the night sky. The other ravens followed.

Mama ducked back behind the willow's branches and leaned her head against the trunk. Rain dripped from her chin. "No matter what happens, I can't let Charlie get the egg back," she said. "I won't."

Then she found a thick branch on the ground and started digging. The dirt was soft from the rain. After she'd been digging for a while, the hole she made gave way into an even bigger hole. "An old groundhog den," she said. "That'll do fine."

Carefully, she put the box inside the hole. She covered it with the dirt. "Don't worry," Mama whispered to me, tucked inside her raincoat. "Horace can finish this. I'll tell him what to do. He will find this and make this right."

You think that Horace is going to dig the egg up and break the curse. No, Mama. Horace doesn't dig it up. Horace didn't make it right.

After she buried the box, my mama left the willow and went back into the storm.

The next thing I saw was the farmhouse. As she climbed the stairs to the porch, the wind and rain pelted her.

I noticed Mr. Pitts in front of a shrub beside the porch. He looked as miserable as ever. I wondered how he got there. Maybe Mama got him from Pearlie Mae's after the curse took her.

No lights were on inside the house. Mama tried a light switch, but the storm must've knocked out the power.

"Horace!" she called out. "Horace! Are you here?"

The house was quiet except for the rattling of the windows from the storm.

She wrapped me in a blanket and laid me in a wooden cradle in the next room. Then she ran upstairs hollering again for Horace. Over and over, she called his name. But he didn't answer.

When she came back downstairs, she lit a couple of kerosene lamps and fetched a piece of paper from a desk. She hurried to the kitchen table.

I watched her draw the map.

"Horace," she whispered as she drew. "Where have you gone to?"

I watched her fold the map in half.

"Where can I hide this so you'll find it, but no one else will?" She ran to the living room. She pulled a book from the shelf, *The Enchanted Tales of French Impressionism.*

The book about Claude Monet!

She opened it and tucked the folded map inside. She went back into the kitchen and laid the book on the table. Then she stopped. "No," she said. "Some place safer." She removed the map and grabbed an empty canning jar from a cupboard under the sink. She slid the map into the jar and sealed it. Then she wrote a note.

Horace—

I know how to break the curse. I buried what Charlie took from the birds that night. I tried to give it back to them. But they wouldn't take it from me. I think it has to be you. You have to return it to them up the mountain. I can't do it.

I made a map so you can find it. The map is in the place where you used to hide from Pa.

I don't know where you are, and the moon is full, and we have to make things right.

For me. For you. For the birds. And for my Cutie. Please, Horace, make things right.

—Your Blue Angel

Mama tucked the note under the Claude Monet book on the table. She checked the clock on the wall. Ten minutes to midnight.

She took the canning jar and ran out the back door to the root cellar. She wasn't in there for more than a minute. On her way back to the house, the rain bit at her face and the wind blew her backward. A flash of lightning lit up the sky. A crack of thunder.

And then there was Horace. He grabbed her arm. "What are you doing out here?" he yelled. His T-shirt and pants were soaked through. His bare feet were covered in mud.

"It's almost midnight," Mama said, frantic. "I left you a note. On the table. Under the Monet book. There's a map."

"Charlie's looking for you," warned Horace. "He's madder than I've ever seen him. He said you took something of his."

Another flash of lightning. A thunder boom.

Mama shook her head. "Listen to me! I know how to break it! You have to return the egg. Find the map and follow it. To break the curse. You have to do it, Horace. Do you hear me? You have to. It's coming for me next."

A jagged lightning bolt lit up the sky. It struck an American pine next to them. The top of the tree blew apart, and what was left exploded into flames. The force had knocked Mama and Horace onto their backs. I saw burning branches brush against the house.

"No!" I screamed.

Horace stirred. He got to his hands and knees. He saw the flames on the roof. The smoke. Then he saw my mama lying still in the rain. He scrambled to her and pulled her into his lap. "No, no, not Magda. Not my Blue Angel." He hugged her head to his chest. Her eyes were closed.

"You can stop it," Mama whispered. "You, Horace. *You*."

"No," Horace said, his voice breaking.

"Take the egg back. Take it to the place. Where it happened."

Horace looked up at the sky. "No, please, no! You can have me! Do you hear me? Take me instead! Take *me*!" The rain came down harder. He leaned over Mama, shielding her. Then suddenly, Horace stiffened. He straightened his back and looked around. "Where's the baby, Magda? Where is she?"

Mama opened her eyes. She blinked away the rain. She saw the house burning. "Cutie!" she yelled, grabbing his arm. "Inside!"

Horace let go of her and ran up the porch steps into the house. Smoke was pouring out of the windows upstairs. He was back outside a few minutes later, coughing. He had me in his arms.

He raced to where he'd left Mama. But she was gone. Neither of us saw the curse take her.

After the memory was over, I let go of the egg and watched it roll into a pile of dirt.

Galen said something, but I couldn't make it out. Because all I could hear was Mama's voice. *You can stop it. You, Horace. You.*

She didn't know that he was already too broken to even try.

All the king's horses and all the king's men couldn't put him back together again.

"Are you okay?" Galen asked. "Because you look like you're going to puke or something."

I shook my head.

"Does that mean you're not okay or that you aren't going to puke?" He picked up the egg and put it back in the box. "This is really weird. I mean, this is the egg that Charlie took from the birds? So this is what protected him from the curse all this time?"

I nodded. It was so unfair. "Everything is hard."

"No argument there." He poked my arm and sort of laughed, but when I didn't say anything back, he said, "Sorry. But look, we did it! You found the egg! The curse is broken now, right?"

"No," I said. "It's not."

Then I told him everything I saw in the memory—everything about my mama taking the egg from Charlie and burying it here, under this tree. About how there was a storm, and how the house burned down, and how my mama was taken by the curse. And how she became a raven. When I finished, he took a deep breath and then let it out slowly. "Whoa."

Anger bubbled up inside me, and tears stung my eyes. "Charlie could've ended it. He could've. He could've made things right a long time ago, and if he had, my mama would still be here. She would've been with me all this time. Ten years!" I shifted the box to my lap and twisted the hem of my shirt tight around my finger. I kept twisting until it hurt worse than the rest of me. "And Horace! My mama told Horace what he needed to do to break the curse. She left him a map! And a note! So why isn't he helping me now?"

"Maybe he can't," Galen said. "I mean, I don't know your uncle, but maybe he just doesn't have it in him to try to change things. Maybe the curse really messed him up, you know? When you see all of your family disappear, and you're kind of responsible, it must mess with your head some. Maybe more than some."

The flutter in my heart came back. I wondered if it was breaking. "I don't know if I can do this."

"The birds believe you can, or they wouldn't have shown you all those memories," said Galen. "And so do I."

"But my mama didn't get any further than this," I said. "If she couldn't break the curse, how can I?"

"Well, for one thing, *I'm* here," Galen said, grinning. "And you've got to admit, I'm a pretty big hero."

"Oh yeah," I said, "your badger experiences are the things of legends."

We both laughed. It felt strange to laugh in the dark when so much awful had happened. But at the same time, it felt good to not be alone.

I reached for the glow of Galen's watch. 11:01 p.m. Only fifty-nine more minutes.

"So what do we have to do?" Galen asked.

"I think everything has to be exactly as it was before to undo the curse. The curse was set when Charlie killed the birds and stole the egg. So to break the curse, I think the birds and the egg need to be back where it happened." Truth be told, I wasn't exactly sure that was right.

"So, um, where's that exactly?"

"On the other side of the mountain," I told him. "Way up. Near the quartz outcropping."

"Oh man, seriously? All the way back up there?" he said, putting his hands on his knees. "Can't you just tell the birds to come here and then give the egg back to them? I mean, they can fly pretty much anywhere, so it wouldn't be asking too much."

I shook my head. I thought about how weak Claude was when we left him. *Even if we get the egg all the way back up the mountain, is Claude strong enough to make it there?* "And there's something else."

"I was afraid you were going to say that," Galen said.

"I think Charlie and Horace have to be there too. In the memory, Mama told Horace that he had to do it. He had to return the egg."

"Seriously?" said Galen. "So you're saying that the people who are after us are the two people who need to be there to break the curse?"

I nodded.

"Just how are we supposed to get them there?"

"Well, they're surely out of the honey-locust spikes by now. And they probably figure we've already found the egg. So, they'll be trying to find us. The birds will make sure they get there."

"And if they find us first?" asked Galen.

"We can't let that happen. We'll have to move our tails. And we'll have to use our flashlights for most of the way. We won't have a choice. Under the canopy, there's not a speck of moonlight."

Galen grunted.

"Or . . ." I said.

"Or what?"

"Or maybe you should go back to your campsite. Or wait here until the sun comes up. It's a long way."

"That's the stupidest thing you've said yet. And between what you've said about the birds and the curse and your destiny, there's been a lot of competition. No offense."

CHAPTER 33

WE SWITCHED ON OUR FLASHLIGHTS WHEN WE LEFT THE WILLOW and kept them on as we followed the creek up the mountain. I kept a lookout for Horace's lantern and whispered Claude's name, and Magda's, into the wind. If they heard me, maybe they would know where we were.

Halfway up the mountain, my arms started to ache. You wouldn't think an egg in a box would be so heavy to carry. But this wasn't any ordinary old bird's egg. It was filled with hope, memories of my family, and probably some magic too. Heavy stuff.

I shifted the box from one hand to the other and kept looking behind me to make sure that Galen was keeping up. He was, but he was struggling.

A yell came from somewhere to the east of us. *Are Charlie and Horace hurt badly from the honey locust?*

"What do you think your uncle and Charlie will do if they find us?" he asked. He was winded, and the words tripped out a few at a time.

"Try to stop us, I guess," I replied.

"I figured that much. But what I'm wondering is, how?"

"It's better not to wonder about things like that." I had been wondering about other things. Claude and the rest of the ravens either hadn't heard me whispering for them or just hadn't come. There hadn't been any sign of them since they'd helped us escape from Horace and Charlie.

Did they know I found the egg? Would they be waiting for me at the place where it happened?

"Are you there?" I said to Galen, keeping my eyes on the steep ground in front of me.

"Here," he answered.

"Not that much farther." My legs felt shaky underneath me. I worried that Galen wouldn't make it up the mountain.

He made an *oomfph* sound.

I slowed. "Want to stop?"

"Yes," he said. Then, "No. I'm fine."

I didn't believe him.

My flashlight swung across the ground, and off to my right I recognized a cluster of white mulberry trees. "We just need to cut straight through, and we'll be there," I said, tightening my grip on the box. "What time is it?"

"Eleven twenty-seven," said Galen.

I told my legs to go faster.

When we neared my rock shelter, I led us east. Not long after, we reached the tree line, and I could see the quartz outcropping. I leaned against an aspen to catch my breath. "We made it." I waited for Galen to say something. But he didn't. "Are you there?" I swung around and trained my flashlight behind me. "Galen?"

There was no answer.

"Galen?" I said again, louder. I held my breath.

"Here," he said, stumbling toward me out of the dark. A low bough of a mountain pine caught him and kept him from falling. "I'm here."

I let go of the air I was holding in. "I thought you might've run into a pack of badgers."

"Funny." And when he caught his breath, he said, "And it's a cete of badgers. Not a pack. So what do we do now?"

I whispered Claude's name into my hand again and threw it into the air. "Hope that the ravens come for the egg." I swept my flashlight in the direction of the rocks. "I don't see Horace or Charlie anywhere."

"Let *me* check." Galen stepped in front of me and scanned the rocks with his flashlight.

"You don't believe me?" I asked.

"I do," he said. "But I'm just making sure."

I waited until he lowered his flashlight. "Well?"

"You're all clear, kid. Now let's blow this thing and go home."

"Huh?" I looked at him sideways. "What's that supposed to mean?"

"Nothing." Galen shrugged. "It's from *Star Wars*. It means, you know, um, go ahead."

"Okay then. What time is it?"

Galen held his watch up for me to see. "Eleven forty-one."

"Ready?"

"Nineteen minutes to save the world," he said.

"Is that from *Star Wars* too?"

"No," said Galen, "that one is mine."

With the box in one hand, and my flashlight in the other, I headed for the rock outcropping. "Come on."

I listened for the birds.

The trees whispered to the sky.

A few steps into the clearing, I saw the full moon. It was more pink now than orange, and it was almost directly over us.

I took a deep breath and started to run. I hoped Galen was right behind me, but there was no time to stop and check.

When I got to the place where it happened, the place in the memory, the birds were there. I heard them before I saw them. Four birds were in a circle with Claude in the center. He was lying on his side in the dirt. *Is he hurt?* But before I could get a closer look, behind me, in the woods, came a crack and a thump. I pointed my flashlight in the direction of the sound. "Galen?" I whispered. He didn't answer. I knew I should go back and find him. He could've fallen or hurt himself. But I was so close to finishing this. The birds were right there, and I had their egg. All we needed was for Horace and Charlie to show up.

I knelt in front of Claude and whispered his name. He lifted his head and then lowered it. I held the box out to him and opened the lid. Immediately, the other birds began screeching.

"Here," I said. "I was supposed to bring it here, wasn't I? Quick. Take it." I lifted the egg from the box and was about to set it down in front of Claude when one of the ravens hopped closer to me and let out a high-pitched shriek. *Rrack, rrack, rrack!*

Galen yelled, "Cutie!"

I saw Charlie first. He was coming toward me up the mountain. His shirt was torn and bloodied, and there was a gash along his cheek. A rifle was in his hands. Then, from the woods, came Horace. He was carrying Galen under his arm like a small dog. "Cutie!" Galen yelled again. Horace tried to cover Galen's mouth with his hand, but Galen was small and quick. He dodged Horace's clumsy fingers.

The ravens spread out alongside me. They puffed their chests and flicked their tails. Their beaks were open wide, and they were screaming.

CHAPTER 34

I SHOWED THE EGG AGAIN TO CLAUDE. "GO ON. TAKE IT. PLEASE. TAKE it and get out of here."

But Claude didn't move. Something was wrong with him. He looked like he was dying. I didn't know what to do or what was supposed to happen next. I clutched the egg to my chest. No matter what happened, I knew I couldn't let Charlie take the egg.

I turned to face Charlie. "I'm not going to let you take this again."

"Don't try to start any trouble, girlie," Charlie warned.

"I'm not trying to start anything," I said. "I'm trying to end it."

"I'll tell you the same thing I told that magpie," Charlie said. "The egg is mine. It's my protection." He looked up at the moon. "Especially on this particular night."

"The egg?" Horace turned toward Charlie then. "The one you took that night? That's what we've been looking for all this time?"

Why doesn't Horace know? Mama told him. Is he so broken he can't remember?

"Shut up, Horace," Charlie said. "I dodged a bullet last time when your sister took it from me. Thought I was a goner for sure. Probably would've been if she'd hung on to the egg instead of burying it like she done. But it came for her instead of me. I might not be so lucky this time 'round."

"If you had given the egg back," I said, "you wouldn't need any protection because the curse would be broken!"

"Shoot," Charlie said. "What makes you think that would end anything? Come midnight, if those birds have that egg, I'm as good as gone. Now, hand it over." He raised the rifle and pointed it at me.

The knots inside squeezed so tight around my

throat I couldn't breathe. I held the egg behind my back.

Then the raven with blue eyes hopped beside me, making low croaking calls. *Mama?* My heart pounded, and I could feel it jumping into my ears. With her there next to me, I felt the flutter in my heart. And the same feeling as before, a fullness.

I didn't want to make myself small and hide. I wanted to protect my mama and the rest of my family behind me. I spread my arms out wide. For the first time, I wanted to be as big as a mountain.

"Do what Charlie tells you," said Horace. He tightened his grip on Galen. Galen kicked his legs and pulled at Horace's ears. But Horace barely seemed to notice.

"Listen to me, Uncle Horace." I tried to keep my voice steady, but it cracked and wobbled. "Magda wanted you to make things right."

"My Blue Angel," Horace said in a low voice, as if he were trying to remember. He screwed up his face. "The curse took Magda. It took everyone from me."

"I know," I said. "It took everyone from me too. But the birds want you to make things right."

"That's a lie," said Charlie.

"You lived in a big farmhouse on this mountain," I continued, trying to hold Horace's attention. "You painted pictures. Remember? You liked Claude Monet and the Impressionists. You were the kind of person who let a raven sit on your shoulder." I wanted to be the string that could pull open the curtains. To get him out of the dark.

Charlie took a step closer. His gun was still pointed at my heart. "You trying to get Horace to save you? You think he's going to be the hero? Is that your big plan? Ain't no reason to believe he's gonna help you."

But something inside me made me keep going. Horace was afraid. He was alone and afraid and broken. And after all the memories I'd seen, I understood why. Maybe Toot was right. Maybe I did have the makings of a luminary. Because right then, I looked through the darkness and saw something I'd never been able to see before. "You wish you could undo what you did."

"It's too late for wishes," Horace grumbled.

"Murderation! It isn't!" I yelled. "Or maybe it is. For wishes. Maybe it's too late for waiting around and hoping for things to change. Or accepting things as they are. But it's not too late to *do* something yourself. Something you know is right."

Horace's knees buckled. He let go of Galen.

"Give me that egg!" Charlie hollered. His eyes were on the moon.

My words were coming fast, like I had been saving them up for years, waiting for this moment to spend them all at once. "Magda believed in you, Horace. She was your Blue Angel, remember? Just like Blanche and Claude Monet."

Charlie looked down the barrel of the rifle. "This is your last chance, girlie."

My outstretched arms were heavy and started to shake. "I believe in you too, Uncle Horace. But you need to decide if *you* believe in you."

If you get a second chance to do the right thing, and let it pass by, is your heart too broken to fix?

"Impossible," Horace said.

"I believe in impossible things. Don't you?"

Then, one by one, the ravens came forward and stood alongside me. Even Claude dragged himself over and toppled at my feet.

At the sight of Claude, Horace got to his feet. In two giant strides, he was beside me.

He grabbed for the egg in my hand.

"No." I fought to keep it. "Don't."

When he took hold of the egg, he turned it over in his palm. For a second or two, behind the deep lines and long whiskers on his face, I caught sight of young Horace—the boy I'd seen in the memories. In his troubled eyes, I could almost see the butterfly flapping its wings. And then every moment that happened after, until this one, when he was trapped inside the hurricane.

So much that was happening right then had happened before. It felt like I was inside a memory watching it play out in front of me. Horace was standing between Charlie and the birds, just like he was that night on the mountain. Back then, Horace had done what was easy. He stepped out of Charlie's way. Would he do the same thing again?

Then Horace startled, like he was hit with a jolt of electricity. *Is he seeing the memory in the egg?* He looked down at the ravens in front of me. He screwed up his face like he was thinking, or remembering, or maybe both. Slowly, he turned around and faced Charlie. "I'm not going to let you do this again."

"What do you think you're doing?" Charlie growled.

"I'm stopping you, Charlie. This time, I'm going to stop you."

"You think you can bring your sister and the rest of your family back? That ain't nothing but a fairy tale."

"It's my fault," Horace said to Claude. "I should've never gone up the mountain that night. It all started with me." His shoulders crumpled like he had been carrying the sky around all these years on his back, and it finally slid off. "It's my doing. This whole curse can be traced back to me. I deserve all I get. So go ahead, Charlie, if you're aiming to shoot someone, let it be me." Horace's body shook, and I worried that he might shatter. He wasn't strong enough. He looked up at the moon.

"Cutie!" Galen said. I looked over, and he was holding up his watch. Midnight.

I felt the wind shift direction. Then I heard the whistle. It was on the wind. It was coming down from the moon.

"Give me the egg! Now!" Charlie yelled.

"Quick, Horace," I shouted, "let it go!"

The whistle on the wind turned into a roar and blew around the quartz boulders and over the birds. It swirled around my feet and nearly knocked Galen down before it got to Horace. It whipped around his head, standing his long hair on end, and it went down his arm to his hand, which was holding the egg.

Slowly, Horace bent over and put the egg next to Claude and the others.

Then he looked at me. A smile was beginning to creep onto his face.

I smiled back. The flutter in my heart felt like something was about to break free. For some reason, I thought about the bird on the disk of the magic lantern that Toot gave me. The one I pretended was stolen by the moon and couldn't get away. It felt like the moon was finally letting the bird go.

The whistle left Horace then and wrapped itself around Charlie. He backed up. He was still holding the rifle. It was aimed at Horace. His finger itched at the trigger.

"It's done, Charlie!" I hollered. "It's over."

"No," he spit. "It's not over for me."

"I'm sorry," Horace said. "We both done wrong, Charlie."

But Charlie wouldn't put down his gun.

Then the bird that was my mama flew at him.

"No!" I shouted. I jumped in front of Horace.

Charlie pulled the trigger. And like a tree in the forest, I fell.

The girl has done it. She has remade history.

With my exceptional assistance, of course.

The burden of the curse slides off my feathers like dewdrops.

And yet.

The cost of my effort has come due.

It takes all I have left in me to lift my head and see the girl.

She's fallen. And she's quiet.

Except for the drumming of her heart.

For the last time, I try to look inside.

Murderation! *as she often says. What had been shuttered now has an opening! A crack big enough for me to see into. This is what I find:*

Longing.

Loneliness.

But I see something else too. It is thin as a whisper, small as a stone, but luminous. And it shines like a star.

Hope.

That's what it is.

I never could resist such a shiny thing.

CHAPTER 35

WHEN I FELL TO THE GROUND, EVERYTHING BECAME AS STILL and quiet as a painting. The whistle and the wind gathered itself up and went on its way. The horizon disappeared. The mountain swirled together with the trees and sky.

History is not your destiny. Uncover your destiny, and you will remake history.

The words in my fortune came to me then.

I lifted my head and looked for Magda. *If history can be remade, then could Mama and the others return?* "Magda?" I said. "Mama?"

I forced my eyes open as wide as I could get them, but I saw only the tops of the trees blurring into the sky. And layers of clouds above them. A couple of dim stars. And the moon.

I found my flashlight in the grass beside me. I switched it on and shone it first on the quartz out-cropping and then on the ground. The egg was gone, along with Claude and the rest of the ravens. Charlie was gone too. His rifle was lying in the grass.

Galen was sitting a few feet from me, with his arms over his head. He was trembling.

Horace was facedown in the grass in front of me.

I reached into my pocket and felt for the heart-beat in my fortune. I waited. I pressed my fingers harder against the words. There was nothing. "But the curse was broken," I said. "They should all be here."

The trees on the mountain were still. They were holding their breath.

A raven flew down beside me. The bird stretched its wings and neck and lay against my arm. Its feathers were smooth and soft. Her eyes were blue.

The bird settled into the crook of my arm, and something passed between us. An understanding. "You can't come back, can you?"

Somehow, buried deep inside, I think I knew it was an impossible thing.

I laid my head in the dirt and stared up the moon. And I cried. The moon seemed to understand.

Galen came over to me. He said my name.

I wiped my eyes. Slowly, I got to my knees. "Uncle Horace?" I looked at his back. He wasn't moving. I crawled to him and tapped his shoulder. "It's over," I said. "The curse is over."

He was still.

"Horace?" I tapped harder.

"Cutie?" Galen said.

I grabbed Horace's arm and pulled it. He was heavy and stiff. "Help me," I said to Galen. "Help me turn him over."

Galen pushed one side of Horace's giant body while I pulled. It was like trying to flip a dump truck. When we got him on his back, I shouted Horace's name.

"What's the matter with him?" Galen asked.

"I don't know." I put my ear to his chest and listened. My own heart was hammering inside my head and making it hard to hear anything else. Had he been shot? I looked him over but couldn't find any blood or holes.

"Oh," Galen said. "Oh no. Is he . . . ?"

I tilted Horace's head back and put two fingers alongside his neck, just like Mr. Desmond had shown me in science class. I pressed my fingers right where I thought the pulse would be, but not too hard to do any trachea crushing.

There was nothing. His heart had stopped.

"No, no, no! I wasn't too late," I said. "The curse is undone."

"Then shouldn't he be . . ."

Don't lose heart. I heard Toot's voice in my head. *Whatever you do, don't lose heart.*

"I won't," I answered. I put one hand over the other, locking my fingers. I put the heel of my hand over where Horace's silent heart was. Then I straightened my arms and started. Down, up, down, up, down.

Just like Mr. Desmond told me to do. I kept the beat.

I remembered some of that Beatles song that Mr. Desmond had played. I sang to Horace about those two people on their way home. I sang as I tried to fix his heart and keep him from succumbing. I kept on singing over and over, stopping every couple of minutes to check his neck for a pulse. Finally, when the muscles in my arms were burning, I felt a faint murmur under my fingertips.

Then Horace opened his eyes. He looked at me. And what he said, in a voice small enough to fit in a pocket, was this: "My Blue Angel."

I started to cry again. "She's not here," I told him. "I'm so sorry. But Magda isn't coming back."

Horace took my hand then and held it over his chest. His heart was jumping. "No," he said, his voice strained, "my Blue Angel." And he squeezed my hand.

CHAPTER 36

WHAT HAPPENED AFTER THAT WAS AS BLURRY AS ONE OF CLAUDE Monet's paintings. Galen and I helped Horace to the shack. We each took a hand and led him home. On the way, the only words spoken were Horace's. "I'm sorry." He said it over and over and over. His words were sturdy and deep as all good sorries should be. I believed him.

Inside the shack, we helped him to his room and onto his mattress. I untied the laces on his boots. Seconds later, he was fast asleep and snoring.

Galen and I walked under the moon through the forest and back to his campsite. We were dead tired, and I didn't feel much like talking. Maybe Galen knew that because he was quiet too.

We sat side by side against the old sycamore and split a pack of powdered doughnuts.

Then we fell asleep. I dreamed of birds.

Horace slept for three days. While he was sleeping, sometimes I sat by his door with Mr. Pitts and read the Monet book to both of them. Galen had given me a bunch of food when we'd made it back to his campsite, so my stomach didn't complain too much.

When Horace finally woke up, I didn't know what to expect. But when the curse lifted, so did the curtain that seemed to make Horace's world so dark.

Like Monet, Horace was still a poor old crustacean and sometimes a frightful old hedgehog, but he talked in straight lines now. And when I asked him about my mama, he told me. "She was the bravest person I ever met. She could fix anything, and just about did too. Should've known there was so much of her inside you."

And he told me about the day the curse took her. After Horace saved me from the fire, he went back into the house and rescued a couple of pieces of furniture, some clothes, and the Claude Monet book. He also grabbed Mr. Pitts from beside the porch.

As for Charlie, there was no sign of him anyplace. Horace went out looking for him. On the mountain. At his house. At the quarry. He heard talk around Gypsum that people saw Charlie leave town in his van, but nobody knew for sure where he'd gone to.

I wanted to believe Charlie Mullet did leave town. That he had just shot his gun into the air on purpose and that he wasn't trying to hurt any of us. I wanted to believe that he got another chance and that he'd taken it.

A week later, all the things in Charlie's cabinet were spread out across several tables at Galen and Dr. Podarski's campsite. I had told Galen about all the things I had seen at Charlie's place when I'd held the fortune. Galen had then told his pop, but he left out the parts about the birds and the curse and my destiny.

Galen was taking pictures of the historical things that Charlie had dug up and was writing something in a binder when I got to his campsite.

"Cutie!" he said, waving me over. "Look at all of this stuff! My pop is losing his mind. He thinks a lot of this was from the site we've been looking for. That Charlie guy was a serious looter."

I carefully picked up a clay pot that had a single crack along its rim. "What's going to happen to all this?"

"My pop's working with the Indigenous people in the state. They are going to have a say in what happens to this stuff. My pop says there's a lot of work to do but that hopefully this will lead to West Virginia recognizing some State Tribes," Galen said. "He's committed to it. And when he's committed to something—"

"'Commitment is what transforms a promise into reality,'" I recited.

"Abraham Lincoln," Galen said, smiling.

"So then people will know who the Fort Ancient people were. And they won't have disappeared anymore."

Galen was quiet for a few moments. He flipped through the pages of the binder and then closed it. "Cutie," he said, "where do you think the ravens went?"

"I'm not sure," I told him. "I tried calling for them, but they didn't come." There was an ache in my chest.

"Oh." He kicked the dirt with his shoe.

Dr. Podarski stepped out of the camper. "Son, in a little while I'm going into town to make a supply run. Oh, Cutie. You're more than welcome to come along."

I looked at Galen.

"Sure," Galen said. "We both will."

"Good deal," Dr. Podarski said. "Give me about five minutes. Cutie, you think about what you need, and we'll get you stocked up as well."

I thanked him and thought about what I needed. What I needed was still a lot. But I had answers for once. And that was something.

When Dr. Podarski went back inside the camper, Galen asked, "How's your uncle?"

I picked up a stone from the table and ran my thumb over its sharp edge. "He's going to be all right, I think. He says now he sees the world with a new set of eyes."

"Thanks to you!" Galen said. "Well, actually, I mean, *me*."

I returned the stone to the table. "You?"

"Remember what I said about the butterfly effect?" he asked.

"Yeah, so?"

"I put a bag of crickets in the principal's office and had to come here with my pop this summer as punishment," he said. "And because that happened, I found the map. And then the birds found you, and you found our campsite. And our food. And you stole it, and then you found the map. And then we found the egg and, you know . . . well, we stopped the hurricane."

"You're saying you're the butterfly?" I asked.

"Of course."

"Because you put crickets in the principal's office?"

"Yeah. In the ceiling tiles."

"What for?"

"Because Lorenzo Aster took my shoes in gym and hid them. He said I'd never be able to find them. But Lorenzo Aster is an idiot."

"I don't get it."

"He put them in a pine tree near the door to the gym," Galen said. "Way up high. So that I'd have to ask for help to get them back." He shook his head. "But all I had to do was shake the tree trunk and my shoes came right down. Like I said, Lorenzo is an idiot."

"Oh," I said. "But what do crickets have to do with it?"

"Word got out around school that Lorenzo took my shoes and hid them somewhere. I never let on that I'd found them. So after school, I got crickets from the pet store, and when the principal and teachers were in a faculty meeting the next morning, I put them, along with my shoes, in the ceiling above the principal's desk. Man, those crickets were loud."

I nodded. "So everybody would think Lorenzo did it."

He scoffed. "And let him take credit for something as cool as that? No way. I confessed."

"You confessed?" I said. "How come?"

"Those crickets were all anybody talked about for the next two months. They forgot about my legs. They forgot about me being different." He was smiling again. "It was the best two months of my life."

"But then you ended up here," I said.

"I'd do it all over again if I had the chance, even if it cost me my summer. Which it did." He elbowed my arm. "So anyway, yeah, I'm the butterfly."

"Or Lorenzo is," I said.

Galen's mouth dropped open.

"Nah." I elbowed him back. "We'll say you are."

Galen moved over to the edge of one of the holes that they had dug. He pushed some dirt into it with his shoe. "My pop says we'll be finished here in a couple of days. And then back home."

"So you can have the operation?" I asked.

"Maybe."

"Maybe?"

"I've decided to talk to my mom and pop about it when we get home," he said. "I don't know what I'm going to do yet, but I want to be part of what we decide."

I looked him over to see if he was fooling.

"Hey, I told you," he said. "I don't lie. I make things up. There's a big difference."

I smiled at him. It felt good to smile.

"So what are you going to do now?" he asked.

It was a question so big that I couldn't see its edges. I reached into my pocket and pulled out my fortune. The printed words were fading, but I didn't need them anymore. I thought a gust of wind might lift the fortune off my palm and carry the slip of paper away. Maybe to be found by someone else who could uncover their destiny and remake history.

I waited for the wind. But when it didn't come, I decided to make my own. I blew the fortune out of my hand in a single breath. It floated in the air for a second or two, before Galen grabbed it. He stuffed it into his pocket.

I looked at him with wide eyes. "Don't tell me you believe in destiny now."

"Okay," he said, shaking his head and smiling. "I won't."

CHAPTER 37

WOKE UP TO THE SOUNDS OF A TRUCK LURCHING DOWN THE gravel lane. A ray from the rising sun found its way through the cracks in the metal siding of our shack and into my room. It warmed my cheek. I jumped out of my bed and yanked off the towel hanging over my window.

Toot was back.

I ran out the door and leaped off the porch. I waved my arms in the air frantically. Toot cut off the engine and threw open the door. "Cutie Pie!" Toot said, hopping out of the truck. "There's my girl. There she is. How I've missed that face of yours!"

I wrapped my arms around her. "I'm sorry." I wanted

it to be the first thing I said. It couldn't undo what I had said to her, but it was the best I could do. "I'm sorry for what I said when you left."

"I know you are, sugar," she said, squeezing me tight. "Now don't you think any more about it." Then she let me go. "Let me have a look at you." She stepped back and looked me over but still held on to my hands. "I was gone a long time."

"Fourteen days," I told her.

Toot nodded. "Fourteen days. That's too long. My goodness, too long. Look at you. There's something different about you. But I can't very well say what."

I nodded. "Let me look at *you*." Her dyed red hair was tucked under a baseball cap. And her eyes looked tired and full, as if they had seen things that were hard to forget. "There's something different about you too."

"We are two different people, I guess," Toot said.

I wondered if that's what happened when you lost someone. "We are," I said.

Toot hugged me again, like if we held on to each other tight enough, we wouldn't lose anybody else ever again.

"Now I want to ask you something," she said, releasing me. "How's it been?"

I felt another flutter in my heart. So much had happened while Toot was away, and everything seemed different now. I hadn't made it to a highfalutin castle like some of the luminaries did in Toot's mama's stories, but I didn't lose heart. And that was something. "Oh. Fine," I said, and this time I meant it.

"Gracious almighty," Toot said. She was looking past the burn barrel toward the shed. "Is that Horace?"

He was standing by an easel, looking at the mountain.

"Come on," I said, taking her hand. I led Toot to him.

Horace was sipping coffee. His face was clean-shaven, and his eyes were bright. Mr. Pitts stood next to him by the easel, facing the sun. His nose still looked boogery, but for once, he had no complaints. And even if he did, I wasn't listening.

I let go of Toot's hand, but Toot held on. "Good morning, Toot," Horace said. "Beautiful sky this morning, wouldn't you say?"

Toot raised her eyebrows and looked at me. "I would," she said, slowly.

I smiled and turned to watch the sun breaking through the sky. "Me too. Very beautiful."

"My fingers have been itching to paint it," Horace said, looking at his long fingers clinging to a paint-brush. "I'm amazed they remember how." Then he brought the brush to the canvas and painted the red-orange scene.

A sunrise.

Later that afternoon, I unlocked the door in the shack that overlooked the deep gorge.

I sat on the doorstep and let my legs dangle over the edge. It was dark, down below. In my hand was the Monopoly car, the metal tube from the paint-brush, and the anchor button. In my heart was the memory of my mama and the family that I now sort of knew.

"Thank you," I said, hoping that the wind would carry my words. Hoping that the birds would hear them. I *thought* they might, but I wasn't sure I *believed* they could. That got me wondering about the difference between a thought and a belief. So I thought about all the things I believed:

I believe in not losing heart.

I believe that a broken world can be put back together. Maybe not exactly the way it was before, but back together in a way that makes things okay.

I believe that butterflies can cause hurricanes.

I believe that if a tree falls in the forest, there's always somebody around to hear it make a sound. And that some-body may be a bird.

Maybe a belief was a thought that came from the heart. Yes, that felt right.

Then I opened my hand and the memories of the curse fell away into the gorge.

Plummeted. Plunged. Nose-dived.

The shack, with one loud creak, shifted forward to have a look.

Moments later, the ravens appeared. Four of them. They flew near me, calling. They were playing a game with a stick. The bird with the stick in its beak flew high while the others chased after it, riding the updrafts. Finally, in a barrel roll back down, the bird let the stick go. The others dove for it until one swooped in fast and caught it. Then that bird took off, spiraling up toward the sun, chasing the light. All except one followed close behind.

The raven with the blue eyes landed on the step next to me.

"Hi, Mama," I said.

The bird leaned into my arm.

"I thought that breaking the curse might've brought you back," I said. "I wanted it so much."

The bird spread its wings and bowed. I understood.

"But Horace seems better," I told her. "Now that the curse has been undone, he's part of this world again. Part of my world again."

The bird pecked at my arm.

Things didn't turn out exactly like I wanted them to. Everything definitely wasn't easy now, but it wasn't as hard as before either. At least now I knew I could see my way through the hard.

"Maybe there isn't just one destiny," I told my mama as I touched her wing feathers. "Maybe we all have a million destinies, and this was just one of them. Maybe there will be a new one tomorrow. And the day after that. Does that sound right?"

She stretched her neck and bobbed her head.

"I forgot," I said. "You can't answer questions."

And then she spread her wings and hopped onto my knee. "Right," she said. Her voice was smooth as a creek pebble.

The world really was full of impossible things.

I watched the three others, still playing the game, get smaller and smaller in the sky. Pearlie Mae and Horace's mother and father.

"Will you stay here with me?" I asked my mama, stroking her dark feathers.

She made soft *gro* calls and leaned closer into my hand.

When he was painting, Claude Monet said that he was chasing a dream and that he wanted the impossible. That's what it felt like sitting there together on the edge of the world, me and my mama. We sat, and we watched the color fade along with the setting sun.

ACKNOWLEDGMENTS

Writing this book felt impossible at times. In fact, for so long I was convinced it would never become a book. I thought its destiny was to live in a desk drawer next to my one-armed Jane Austen action figure and broken Pez dispensers. But sometimes things that feel impossible aren't so much.

Here's what *is* impossible: bringing a book into the world all by yourself. Which is why I am so grateful for all of the people who helped me along the way.

Thank you to my family, especially my mom, who is one of the strongest women I know. Despite having a really rough couple of years, she always managed to ask, "How's that raven book coming along?" And to my sister, Heidi, who is full of all the good kind of magic and who inspires me every day to find joy in small things.

Andy, thank you for believing in me and giving me space to write (and rewrite). And for patiently answering all of my archaeology-related questions. And for buying me a proper desk chair. And raven-type things. And for your love. Mostly for that, thank you.

Opal, thank you for asking about my stories and offering ways to make them better. You have the makings of a luminary, and your light shines brighter than the sun.

Thanks to so many who read early, ugly drafts (sometimes more than once): Tim Wynne-Jones, Annemarie O'Brien, Elissa Brent Weissman, Elisabeth Dahl, Lori Steel, Erin Hagar, Jade Keller, and Linden McNeilly.

Thank you to Yasmin Kloth for your midday chickens and your encouragement, especially on dark days. Your poet's soul is magnificent.

Thank you, Sarah Davies, for not giving up on me or Cutie. And thanks to the rest of the Greenhouse team for your support.

Catherine Frank, you are a dream editor, and I'm

so grateful for your kindness and patience and eye for detail. Through all of the drafts, you helped me not to lose heart. You helped me find the story I wanted to tell.

Thanks to Margaret Quinlin, Lily Steele, Adela Pons, and the rest of the incredible team at Peachtree.

Thank you, Rebecca Behrens, for your mad copy-editing skills, and thank you, Alona Millgram, for your gorgeously moody cover art.

Thanks to Vermont College of Fine Arts MFA program, and the wonderful writing community it fosters.

Thank you to Dr. Philip McClure at the International Center for Limb Lengthening, Rubin Institute for Advanced Orthopedics, and to Eleanor Morris at the Children's Hospital at Westmead for your generosity in answering all my questions about fibular hemimelia. Also thanks to Joshua Pate, PhD, Macquarie University, Faculty of Medicine & Health Sciences.

The book *Mad Enchantment: Claude Monet and the Painting of the Water Lilies* by Ross King taught me so much about the life, work, and anguish of Mr. Monet. Thank you, Mr. King, for writing it. Likewise, the book

Mind of the Raven: Investigations and Adventures with Wolf-Birds by Bernd Heinrich is a fascinating journey into the life and behavior of ravens.

Thanks to the Cornell Lab of Ornithology and their many scientists who work to understand and protect birds and the natural world.

Thank you to the staff and volunteers at Share Our Strength and No Kid Hungry, who work to give the more than 13 million food-insecure kids in the United States access to child nutrition programs.

Thank you, Fiona Robinson, for your beautiful artwork of ravens in a tree, which helped inspire this story.

Thank you to the raven who visited me on the porch that one afternoon. I named you Lenore and offered to knit you a sweater if you visited a bit longer. But you had other things to do. I understand. You're busy. Maybe some other time.

And for you, readers, teachers, and librarians. Thank you for picking up this book. You help make impossible things possible.

ABOUT
Shawn K. Stout

Shawn K. Stout grew up a stone's throw from the mountains of West Virginia, where she spent many days wandering in the woods and staring up at the clouds. She is the author of several acclaimed books for young readers, including the Penelope Crumb series and the historical novel *A Tiny Piece of Sky*. Shawn is a science writer at the National Institutes of Health and holds an MFA in writing from Vermont College of Fine Arts. She lives with her husband and daughter (as well as a brood of hens, a pack of dogs, a consortium of hermit crabs, a troubling of goldfish, and a donsy of garden gnomes) in a very old house in Maryland, where she sets out trinkets for birds just in case. Visit her at *ShawnKStout.com*.